The Little Mermaid

Adapted by

METAPHROG

Based on the tale by

HANS CHRISTIAN ANDERSEN

PAPERCUTZ™

New York

Hans Christian Andersen's

THE LITTLE MERMAID

by Metaphrog

Dawn Guzzo — Production
Sasha Kimiatek — Production Coordinator
Jeff Whitman — Assistant Managing Editor
Jim Salicrup
Editor-in-Chief

ISBN: 978-1-62991-739-9

 The author acknowledges support from Creative Scotland towards the creation of this book.

Papercutz books may be purchased for business or promotional use. For information on bulk purchases please contact Macmillan Corporate and Premium Sales Department at (800) 221-7945 x5442.

Printed in China. April 2017 by WKT Co. Ltd.

Distributed by Macmillan
First Printing

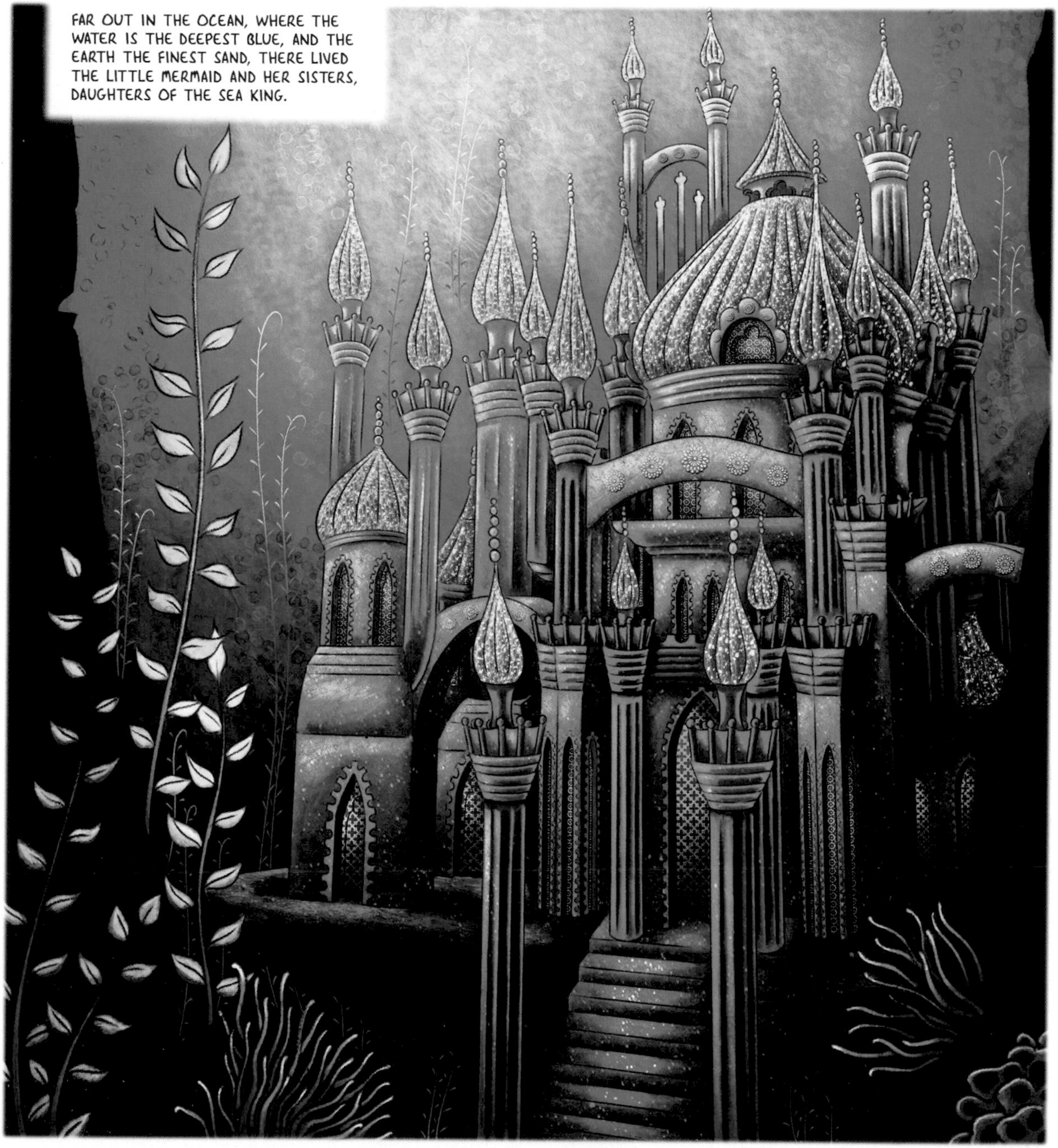
FAR OUT IN THE OCEAN, WHERE THE WATER IS THE DEEPEST BLUE, AND THE EARTH THE FINEST SAND, THERE LIVED THE LITTLE MERMAID AND HER SISTERS, DAUGHTERS OF THE SEA KING.

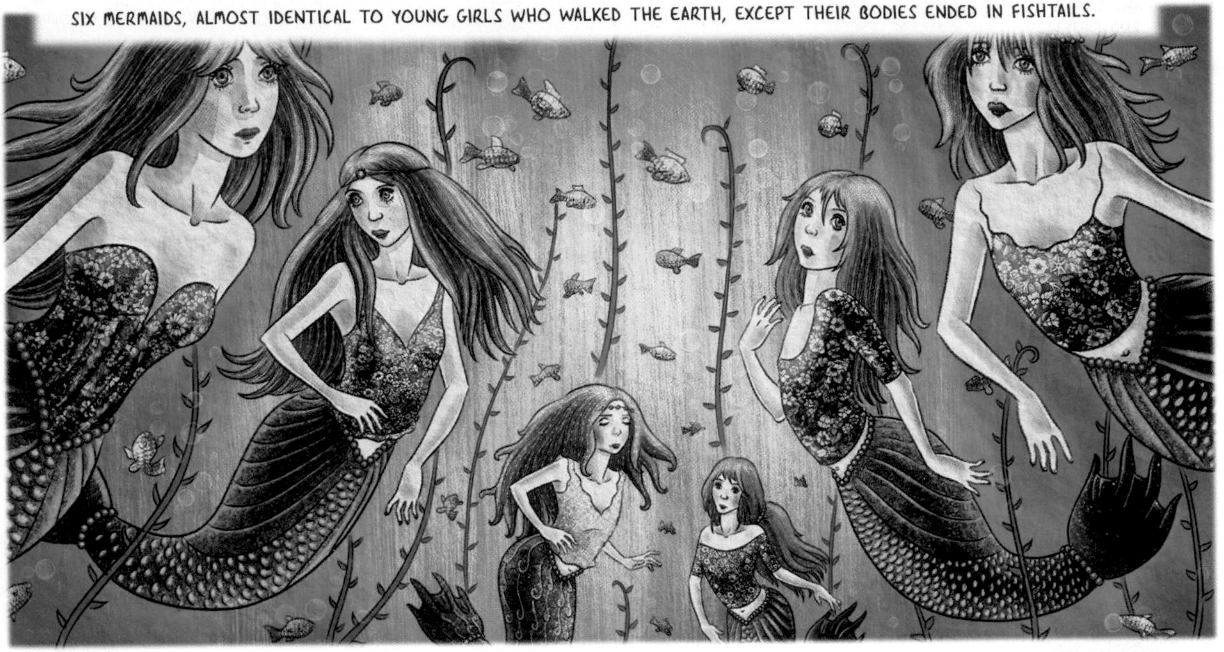
SIX MERMAIDS, ALMOST IDENTICAL TO YOUNG GIRLS WHO WALKED THE EARTH, EXCEPT THEIR BODIES ENDED IN FISHTAILS.

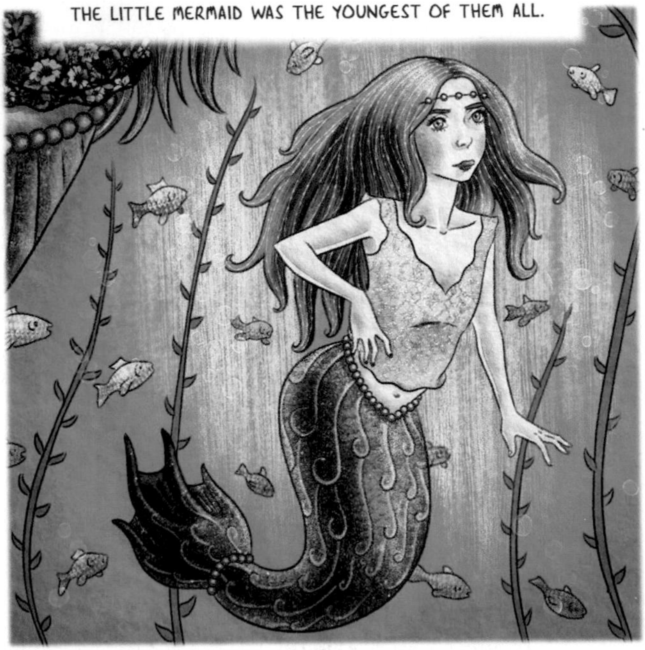
THE LITTLE MERMAID WAS THE YOUNGEST OF THEM ALL.

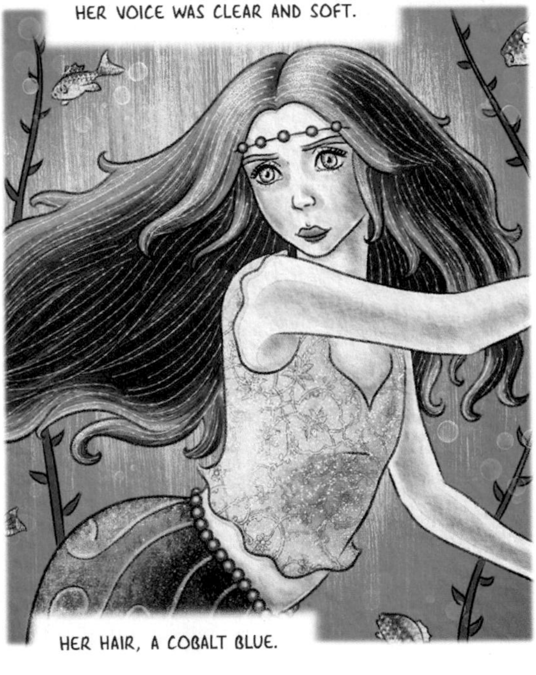
HER VOICE WAS CLEAR AND SOFT.
HER HAIR, A COBALT BLUE.

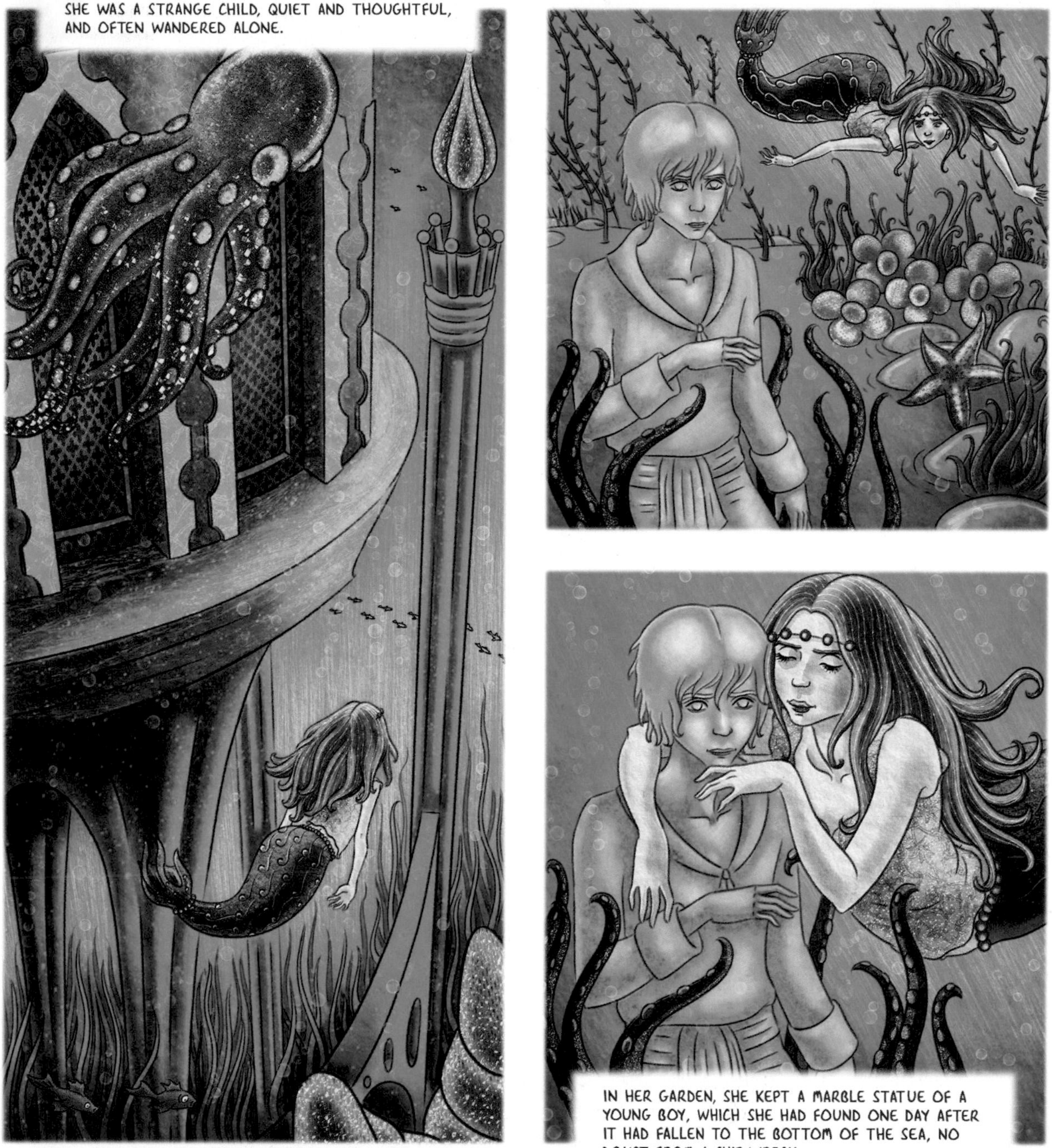
SHE WAS A STRANGE CHILD, QUIET AND THOUGHTFUL, AND OFTEN WANDERED ALONE.
IN HER GARDEN, SHE KEPT A MARBLE STATUE OF A YOUNG BOY, WHICH SHE HAD FOUND ONE DAY AFTER IT HAD FALLEN TO THE BOTTOM OF THE SEA, NO DOUBT FROM A SHIP-WRECK.

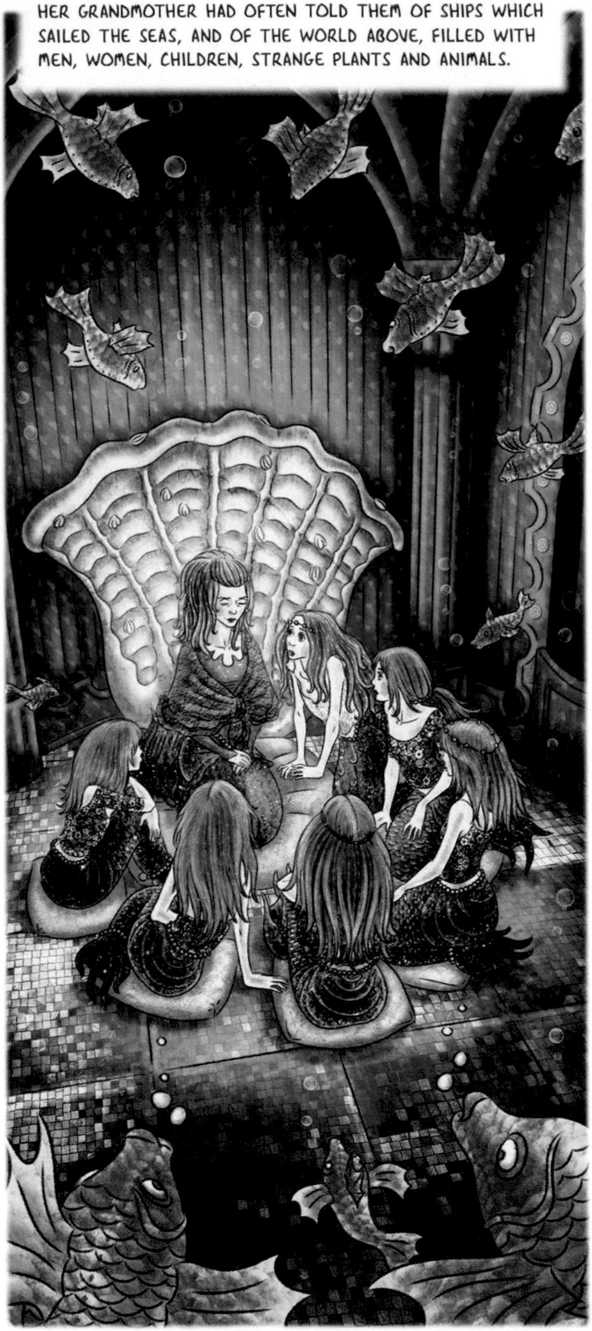
HER GRANDMOTHER HAD OFTEN TOLD THEM OF SHIPS WHICH SAILED THE SEAS, AND OF THE WORLD ABOVE, FILLED WITH MEN, WOMEN, CHILDREN, STRANGE PLANTS AND ANIMALS.

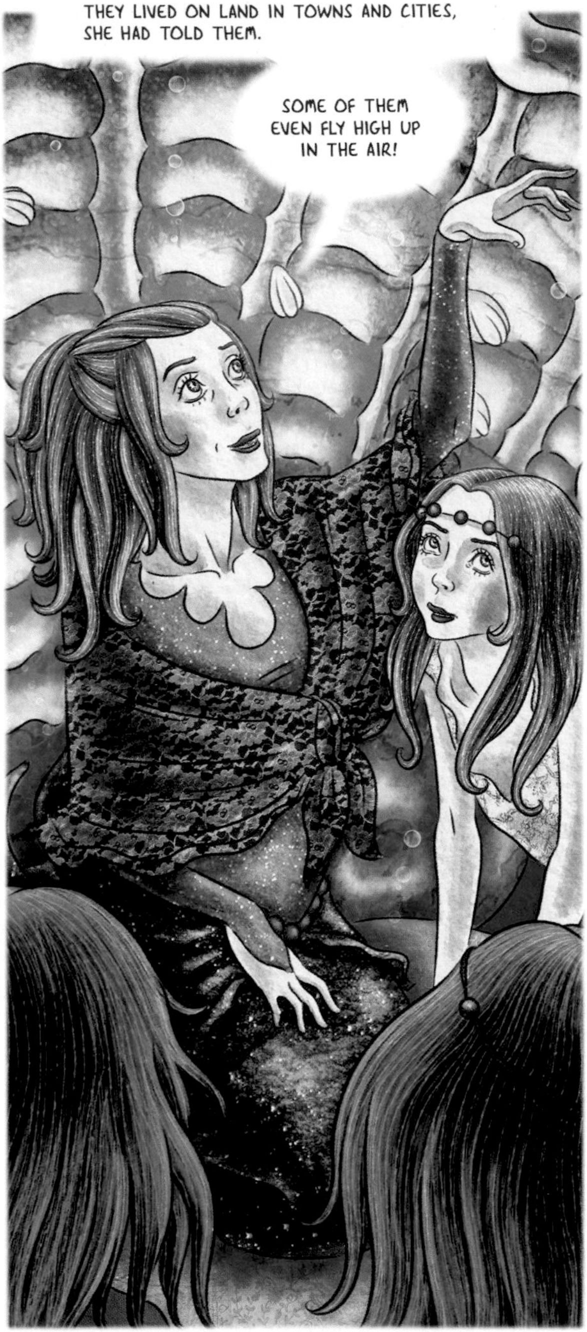
THEY LIVED ON LAND IN TOWNS AND CITIES, SHE HAD TOLD THEM.
SOME OF THEM EVEN FLY HIGH UP IN THE AIR!

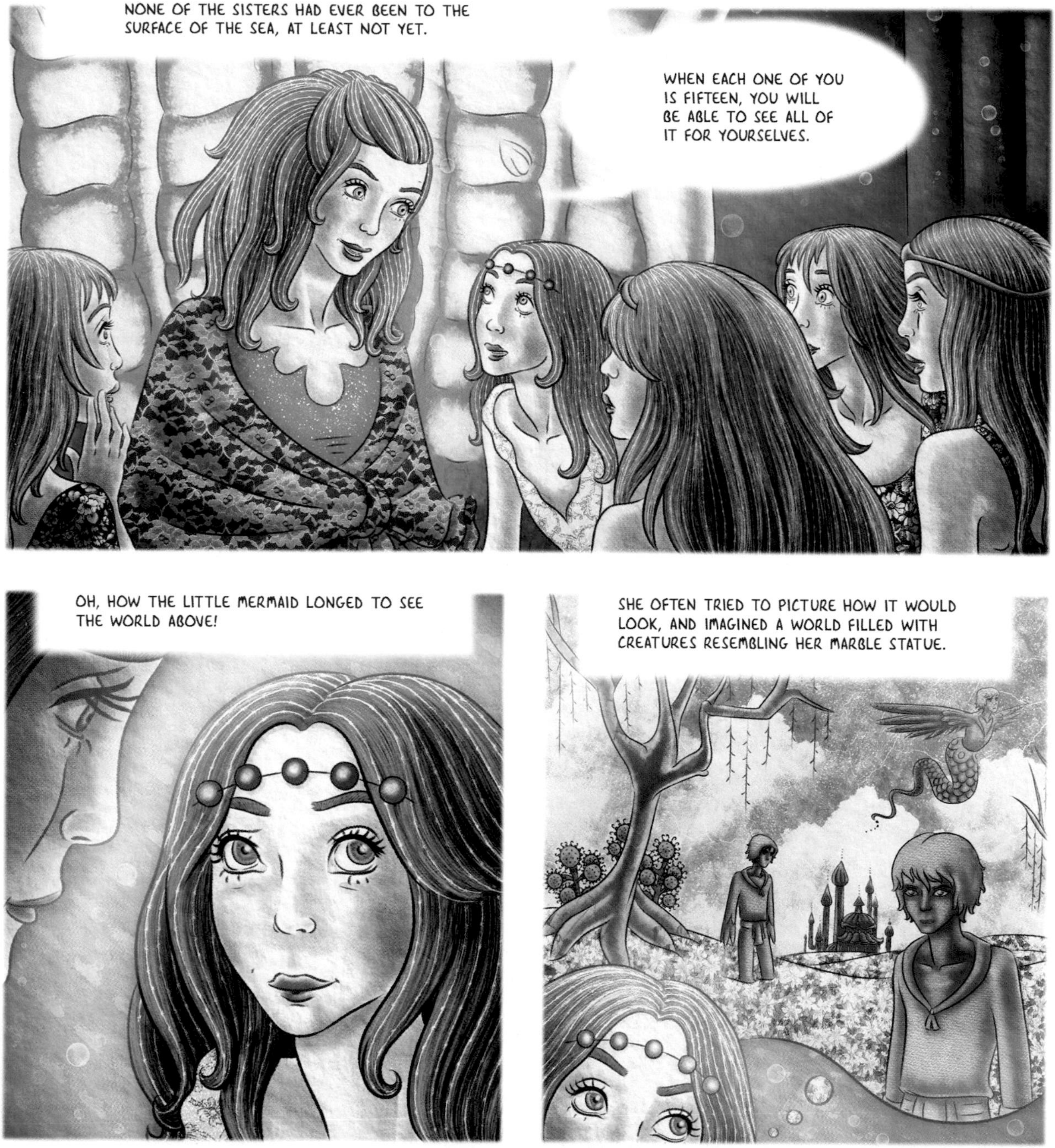
NONE OF THE SISTERS HAD EVER BEEN TO THE SURFACE OF THE SEA, AT LEAST NOT YET.
WHEN EACH ONE OF YOU IS FIFTEEN, YOU WILL BE ABLE TO SEE ALL OF IT FOR YOURSELVES.
OH, HOW THE LITTLE MERMAID LONGED TO SEE THE WORLD ABOVE!
SHE OFTEN TRIED TO PICTURE HOW IT WOULD LOOK, AND IMAGINED A WORLD FILLED WITH CREATURES RESEMBLING HER MARBLE STATUE.

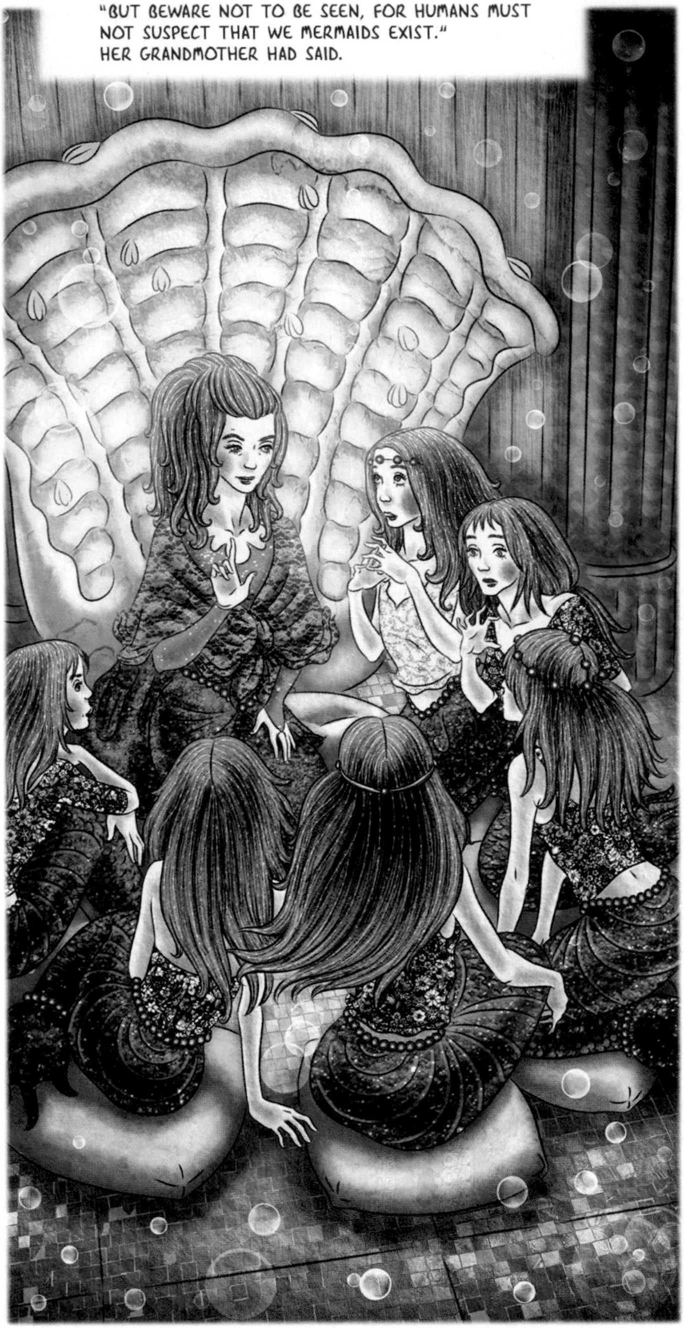
"BUT BEWARE NOT TO BE SEEN, FOR HUMANS MUST NOT SUSPECT THAT WE MERMAIDS EXIST."
HER GRANDMOTHER HAD SAID.

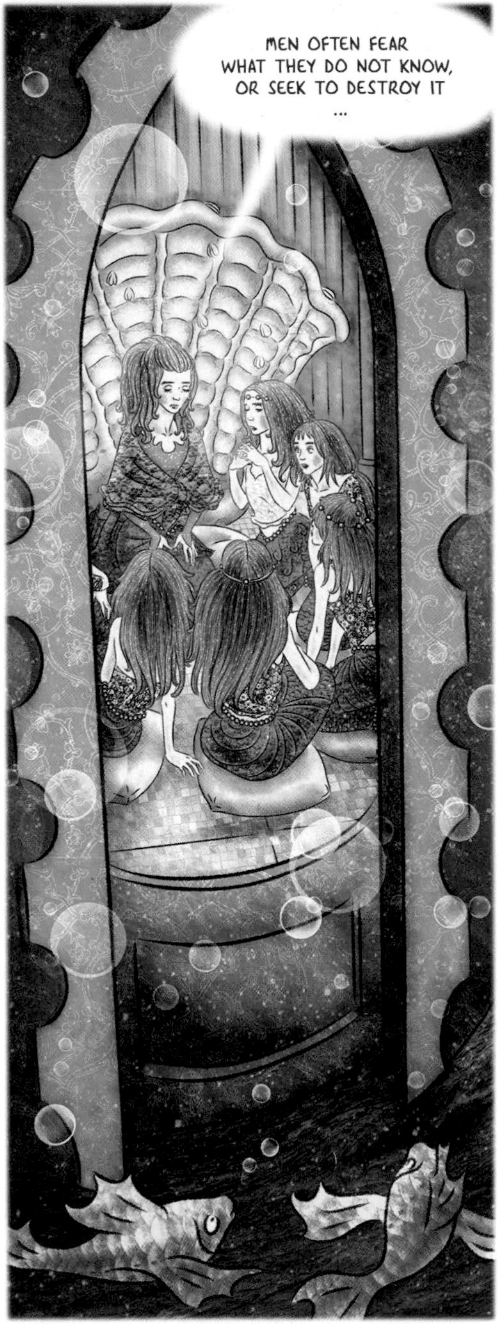
MEN OFTEN FEAR WHAT THEY DO NOT KNOW, OR SEEK TO DESTROY IT ...

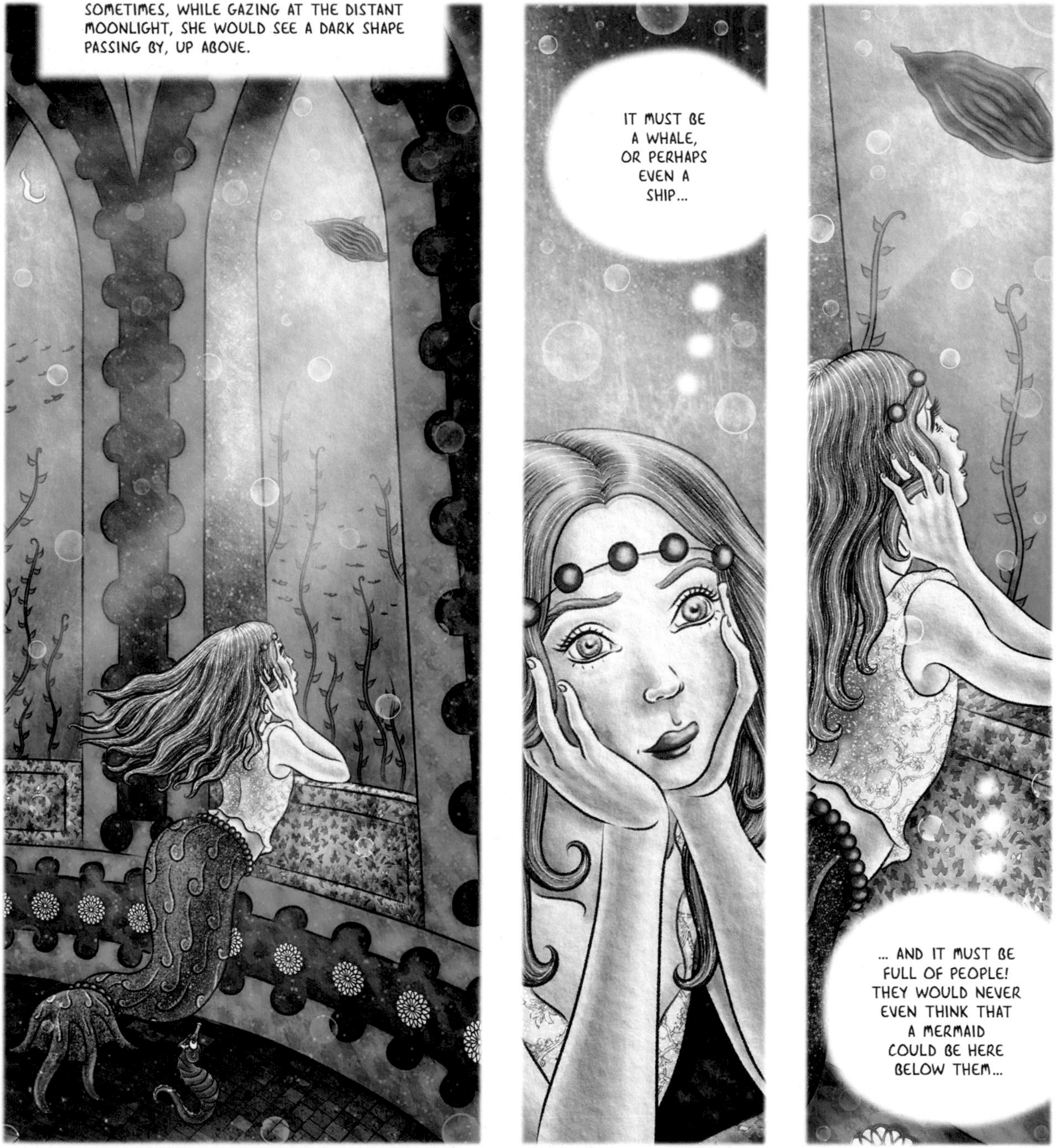
SOMETIMES, WHILE GAZING AT THE DISTANT MOONLIGHT, SHE WOULD SEE A DARK SHAPE PASSING BY, UP ABOVE.
IT MUST BE A WHALE, OR PERHAPS EVEN A SHIP...
... AND IT MUST BE FULL OF PEOPLE! THEY WOULD NEVER EVEN THINK THAT A MERMAID COULD BE HERE BELOW THEM...

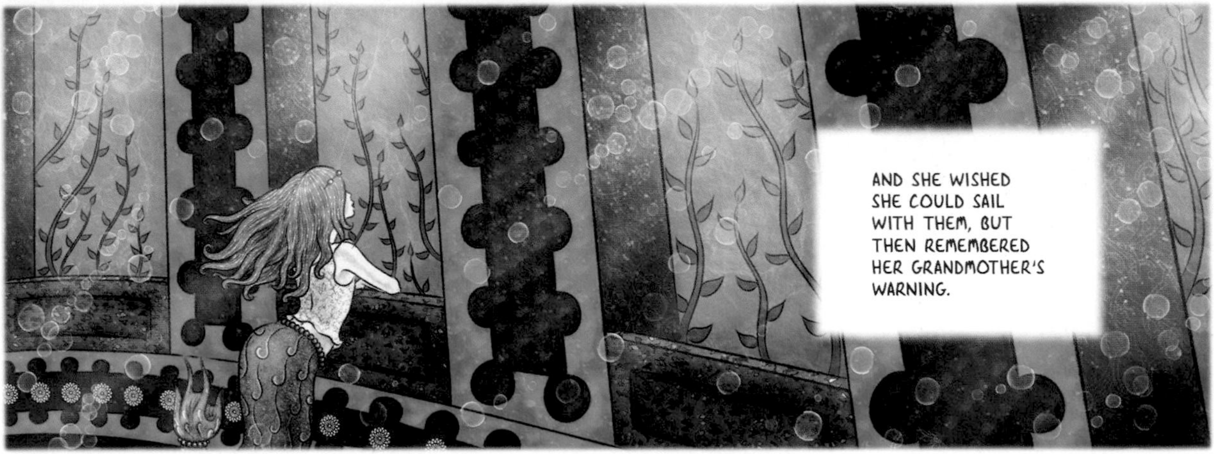
AND SHE WISHED SHE COULD SAIL WITH THEM, BUT THEN REMEMBERED HER GRANDMOTHER'S WARNING.

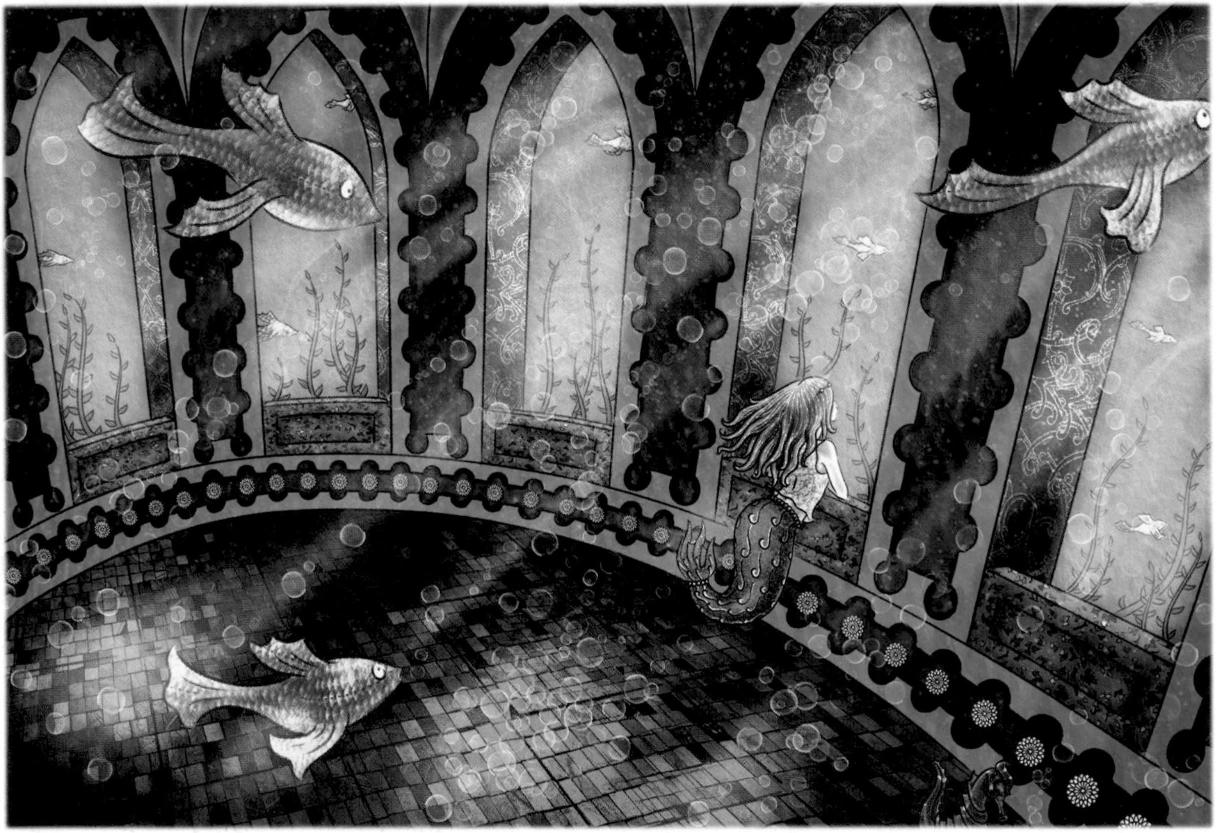

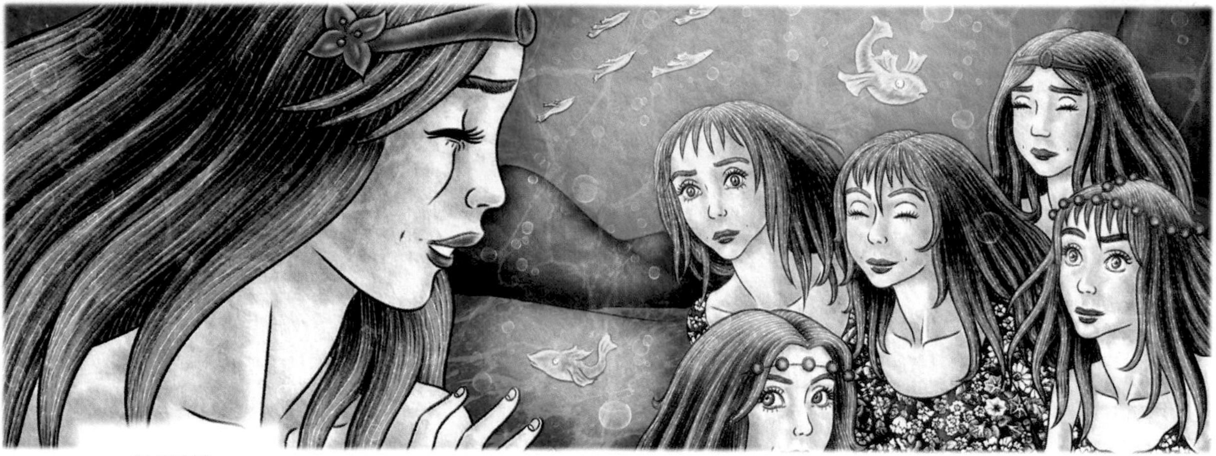

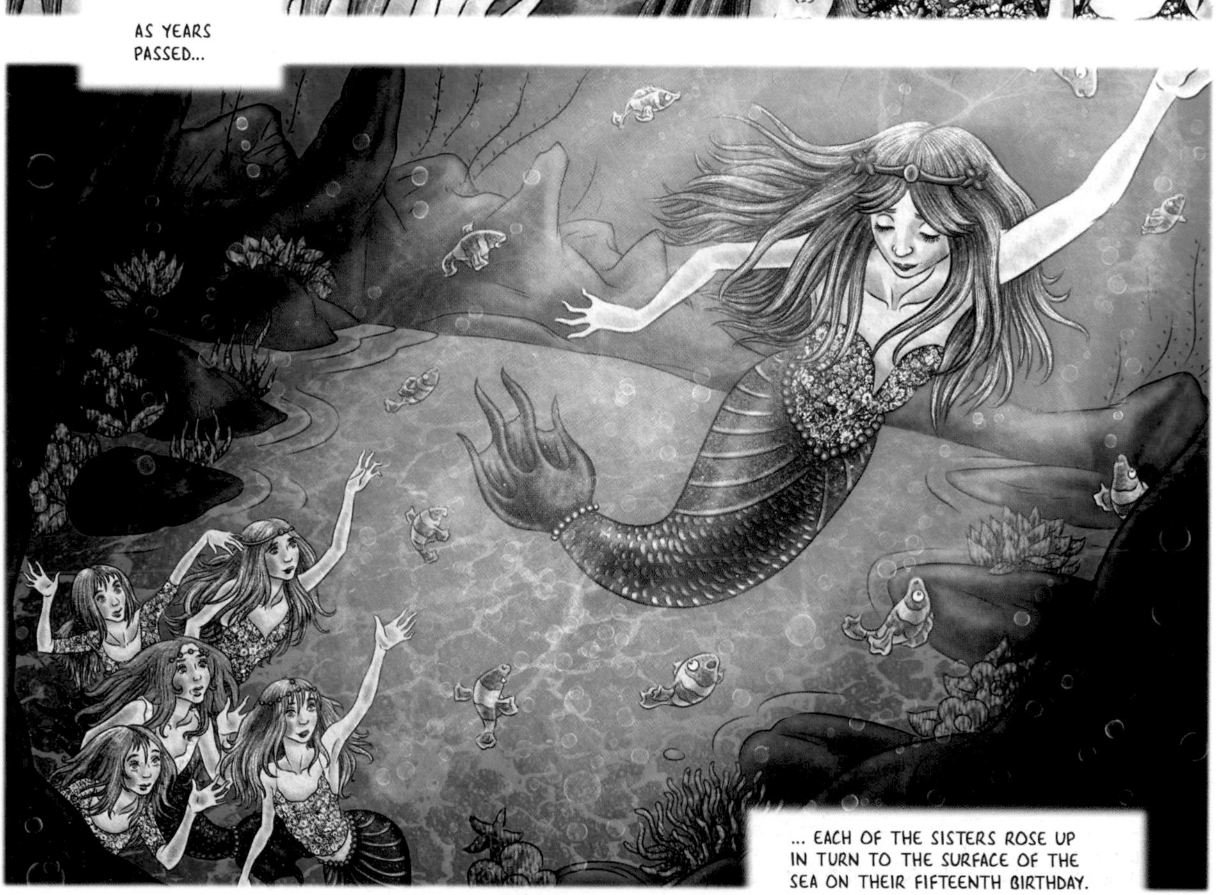
AS YEARS PASSED...
... EACH OF THE SISTERS ROSE UP IN TURN TO THE SURFACE OF THE SEA ON THEIR FIFTEENTH BIRTHDAY.

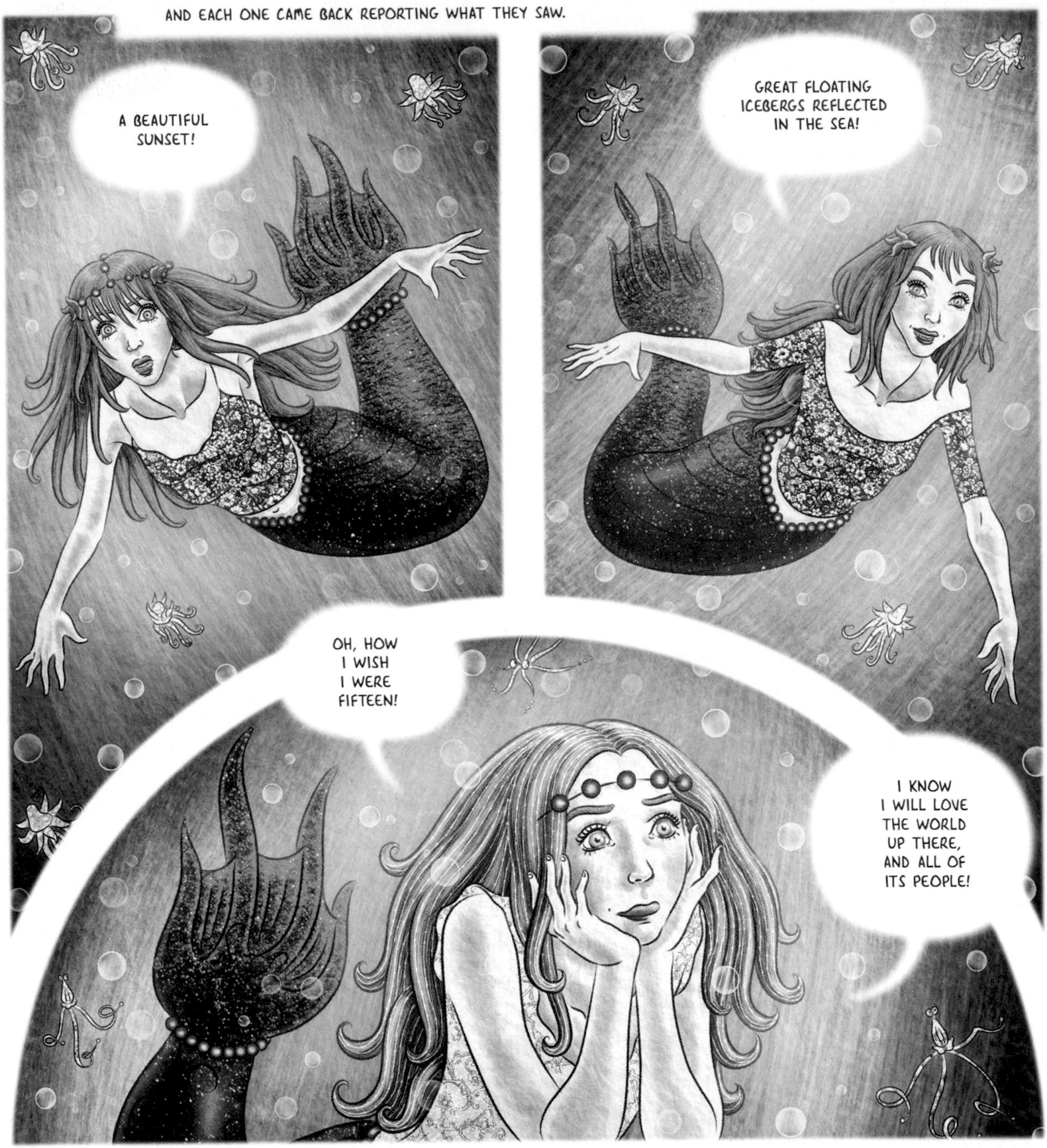
AND EACH ONE CAME BACK REPORTING WHAT THEY SAW.
A BEAUTIFUL SUNSET!
GREAT FLOATING ICEBERGS REFLECTED IN THE SEA!
OH, HOW I WISH I WERE FIFTEEN!
I KNOW I WILL LOVE THE WORLD UP THERE, AND ALL OF ITS PEOPLE!

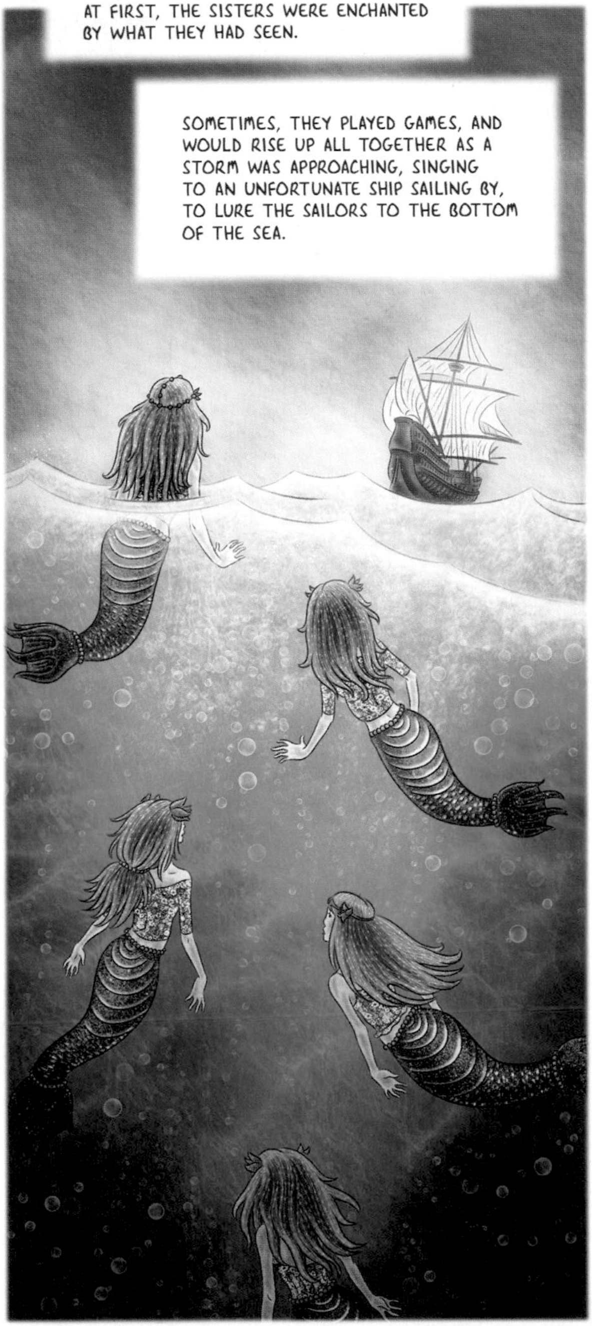
AT FIRST, THE SISTERS WERE ENCHANTED BY WHAT THEY HAD SEEN.
SOMETIMES, THEY PLAYED GAMES, AND WOULD RISE UP ALL TOGETHER AS A STORM WAS APPROACHING, SINGING TO AN UNFORTUNATE SHIP SAILING BY, TO LURE THE SAILORS TO THE BOTTOM OF THE SEA.

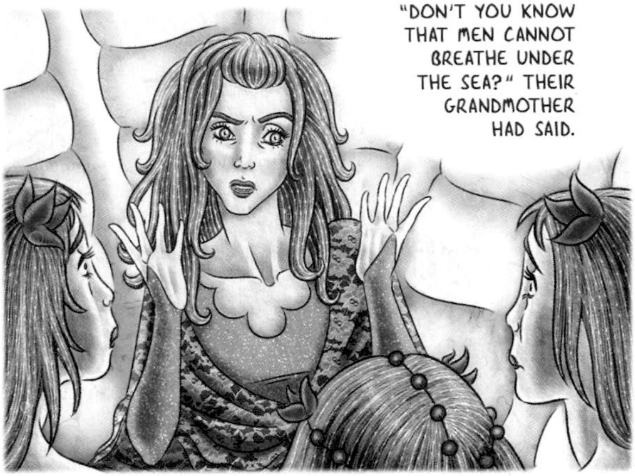
"DON'T YOU KNOW THAT MEN CANNOT BREATHE UNDER THE SEA?" THEIR GRANDMOTHER HAD SAID.

THE SISTERS HAD NOT REALISED THAT IF A SHIP SANK, THE SAILORS WOULD ALL BE DROWNED.

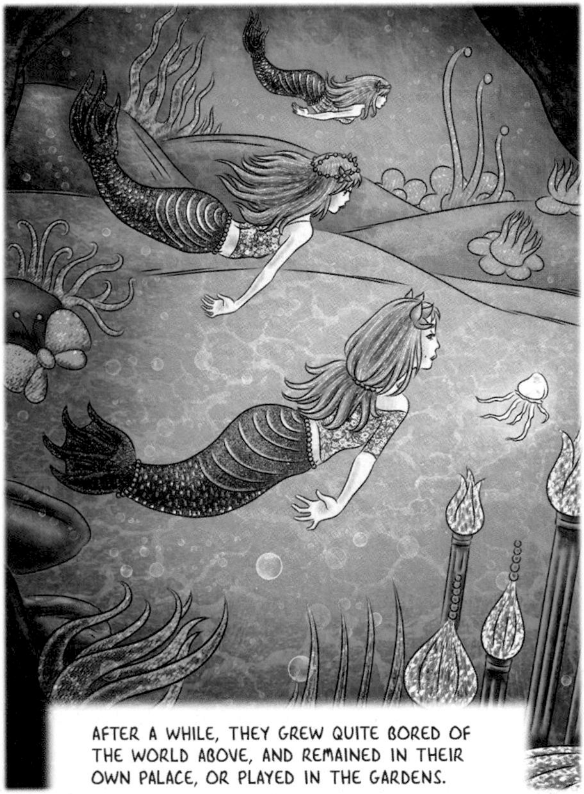
AFTER A WHILE, THEY GREW QUITE BORED OF THE WORLD ABOVE, AND REMAINED IN THEIR OWN PALACE, OR PLAYED IN THE GARDENS.

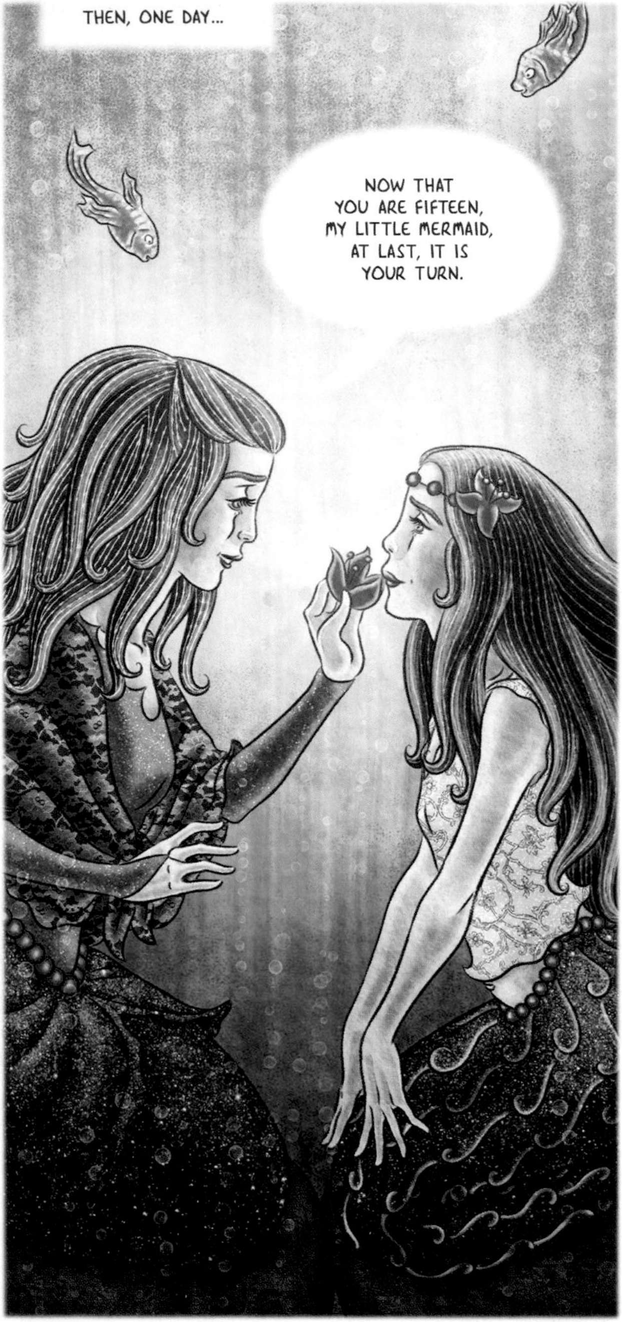
THEN, ONE DAY...
NOW THAT YOU ARE FIFTEEN, MY LITTLE MERMAID, AT LAST, IT IS YOUR TURN.

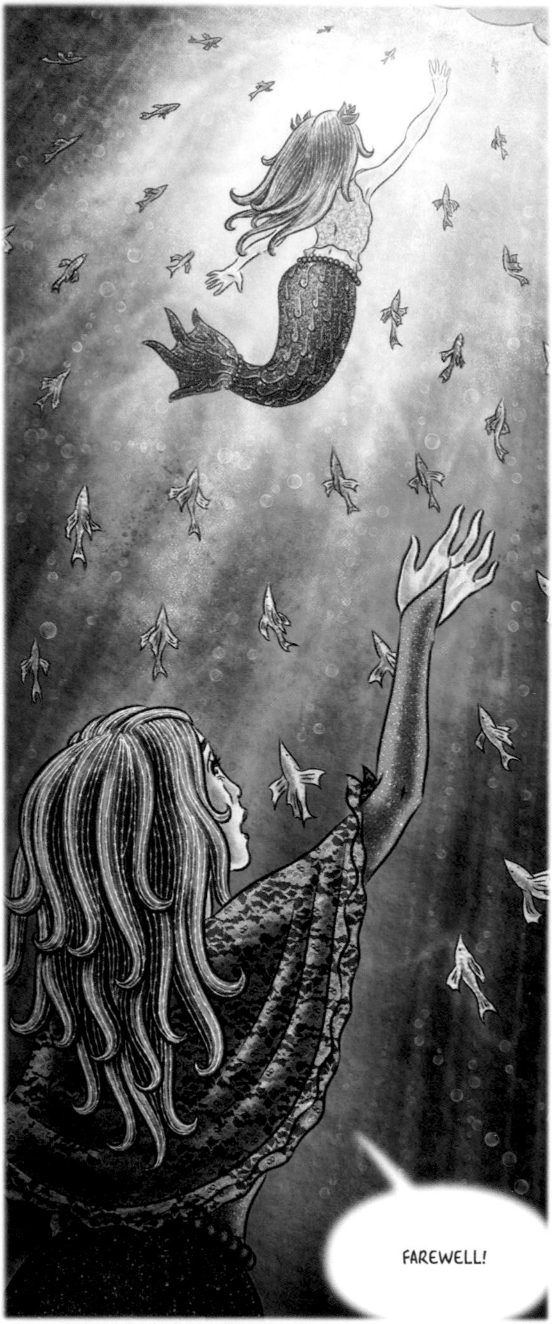
FAREWELL!

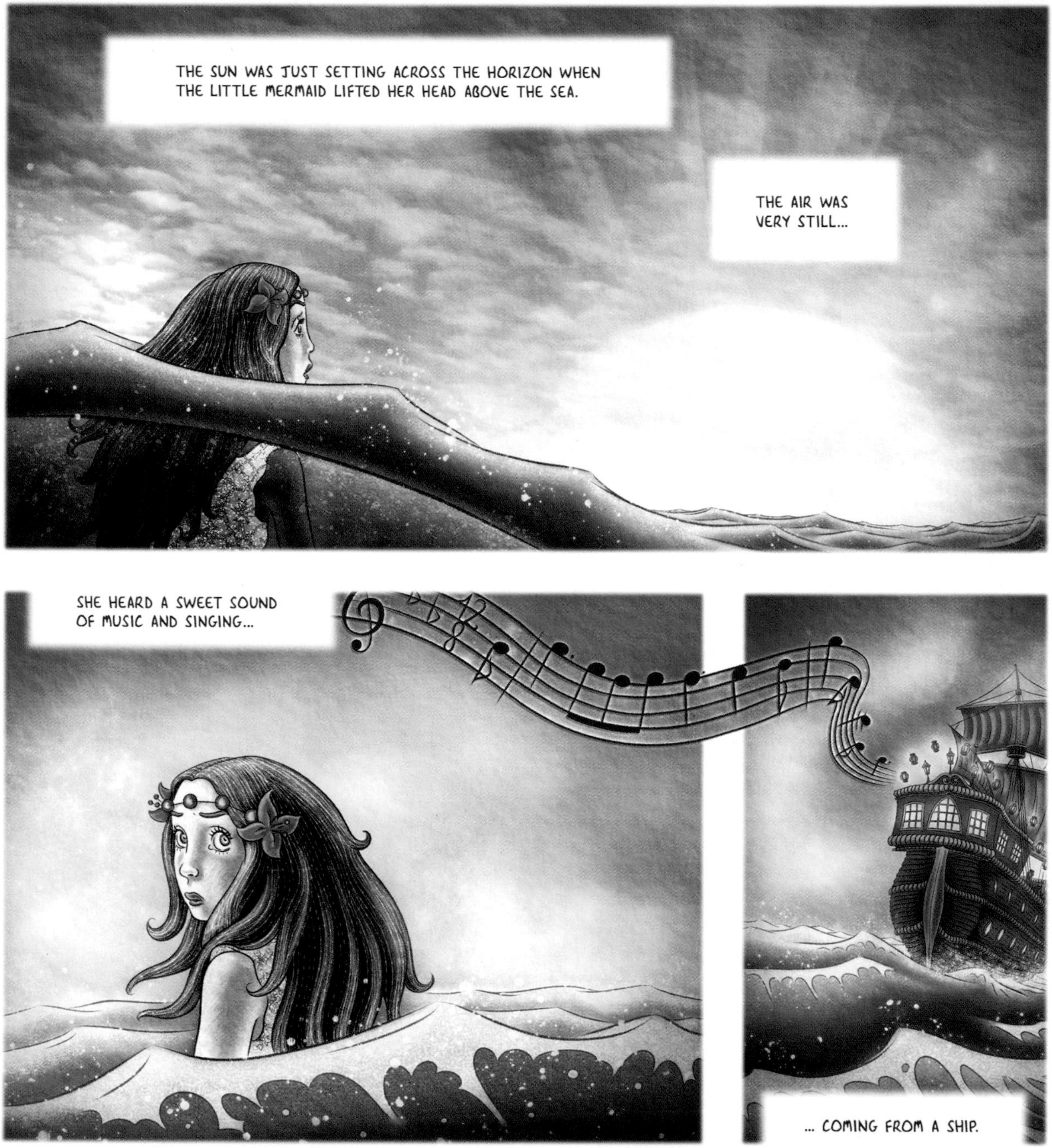
THE SUN WAS JUST SETTING ACROSS THE HORIZON WHEN THE LITTLE MERMAID LIFTED HER HEAD ABOVE THE SEA.
THE AIR WAS VERY STILL...
SHE HEARD A SWEET SOUND OF MUSIC AND SINGING...
... COMING FROM A SHIP.

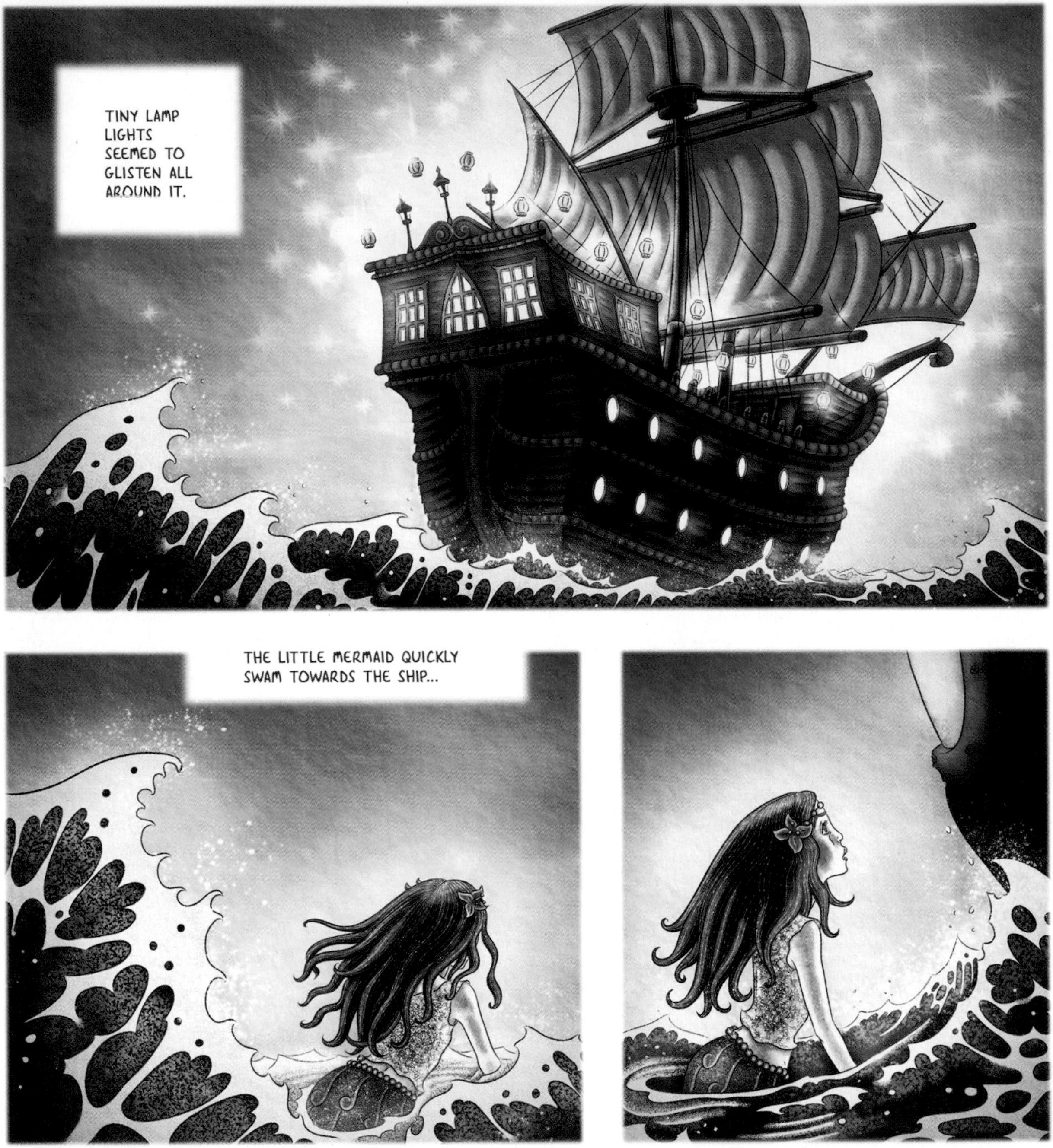
TINY LAMP LIGHTS SEEMED TO GLISTEN ALL AROUND IT.
THE LITTLE MERMAID QUICKLY SWAM TOWARDS THE SHIP...

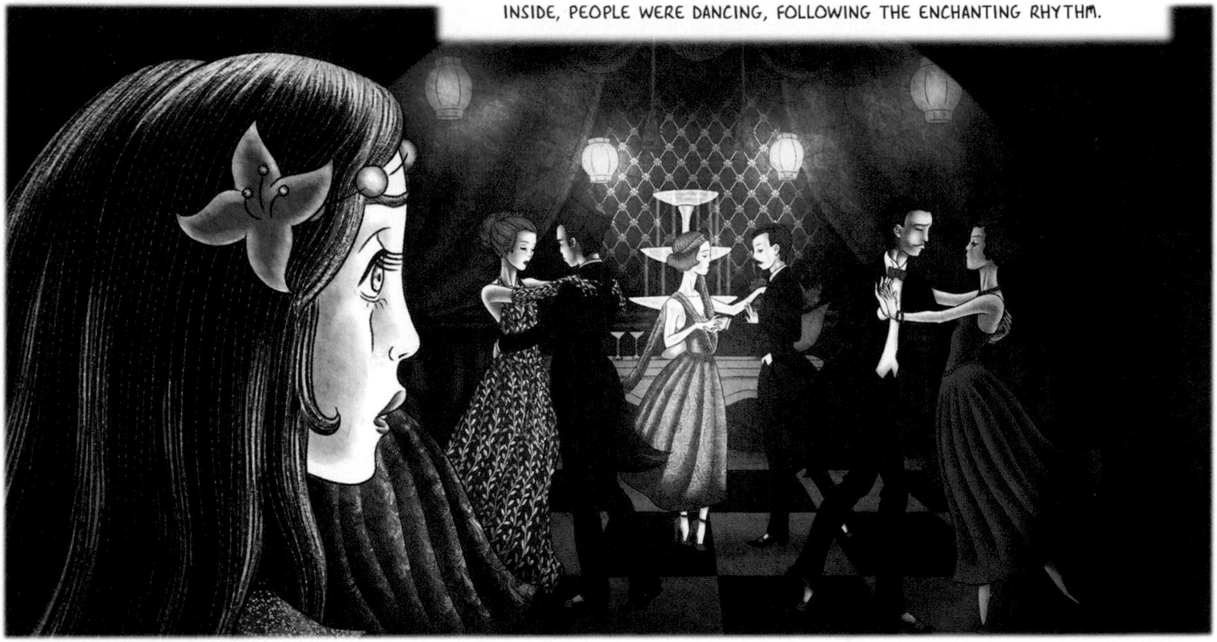
INSIDE, PEOPLE WERE DANCING, FOLLOWING THE ENCHANTING RHYTHM.

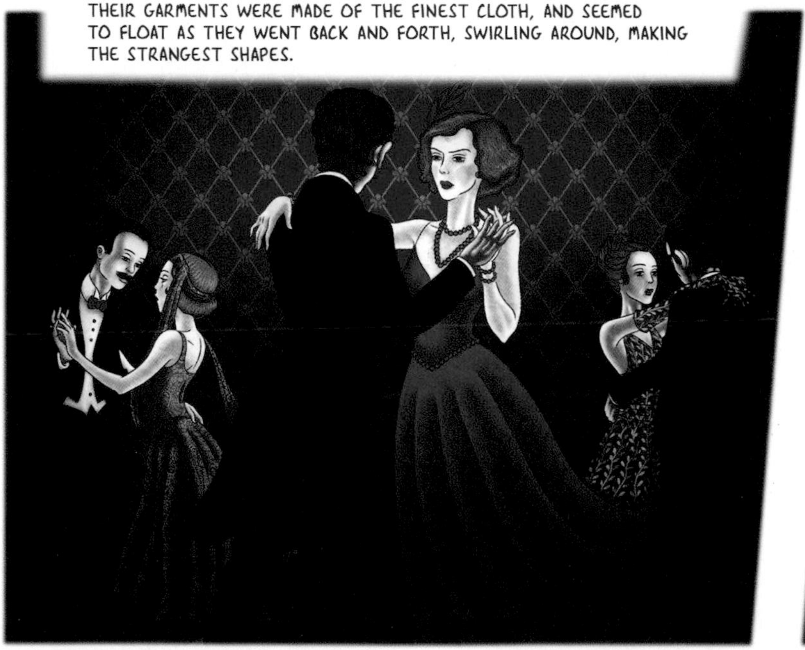
THEIR GARMENTS WERE MADE OF THE FINEST CLOTH, AND SEEMED TO FLOAT AS THEY WENT BACK AND FORTH, SWIRLING AROUND, MAKING THE STRANGEST SHAPES.

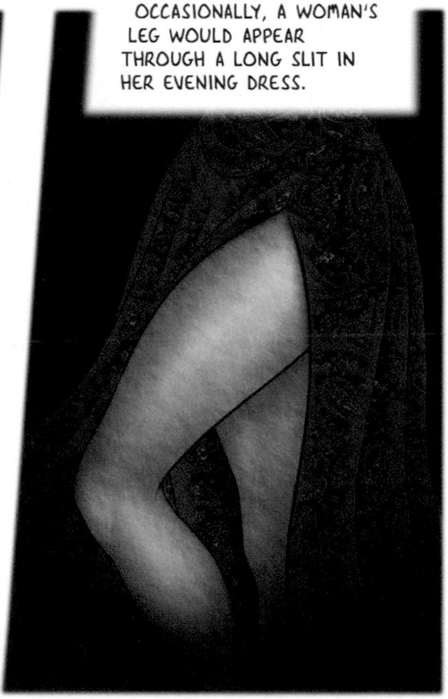
OCCASIONALLY, A WOMAN'S LEG WOULD APPEAR THROUGH A LONG SLIT IN HER EVENING DRESS.

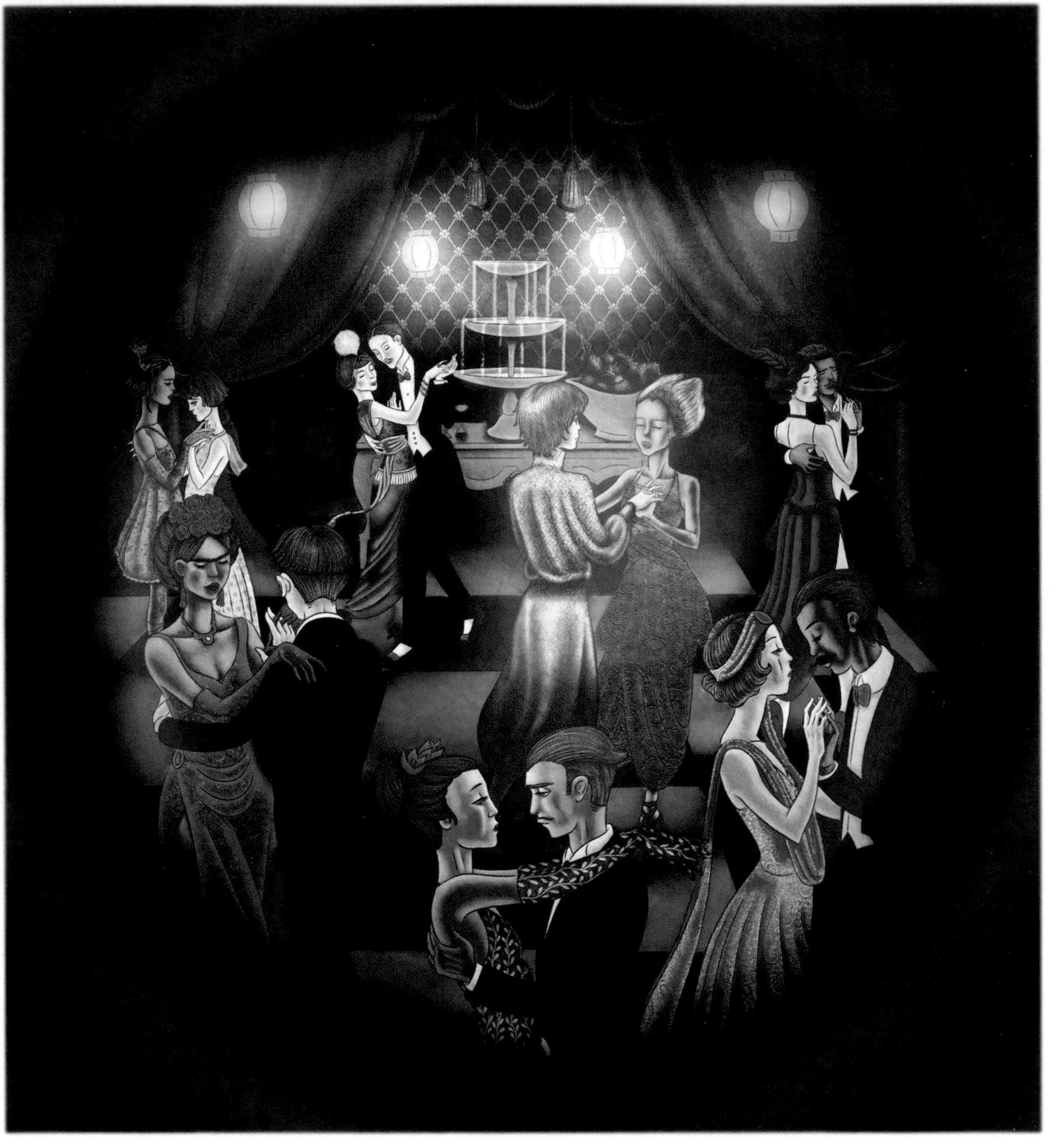

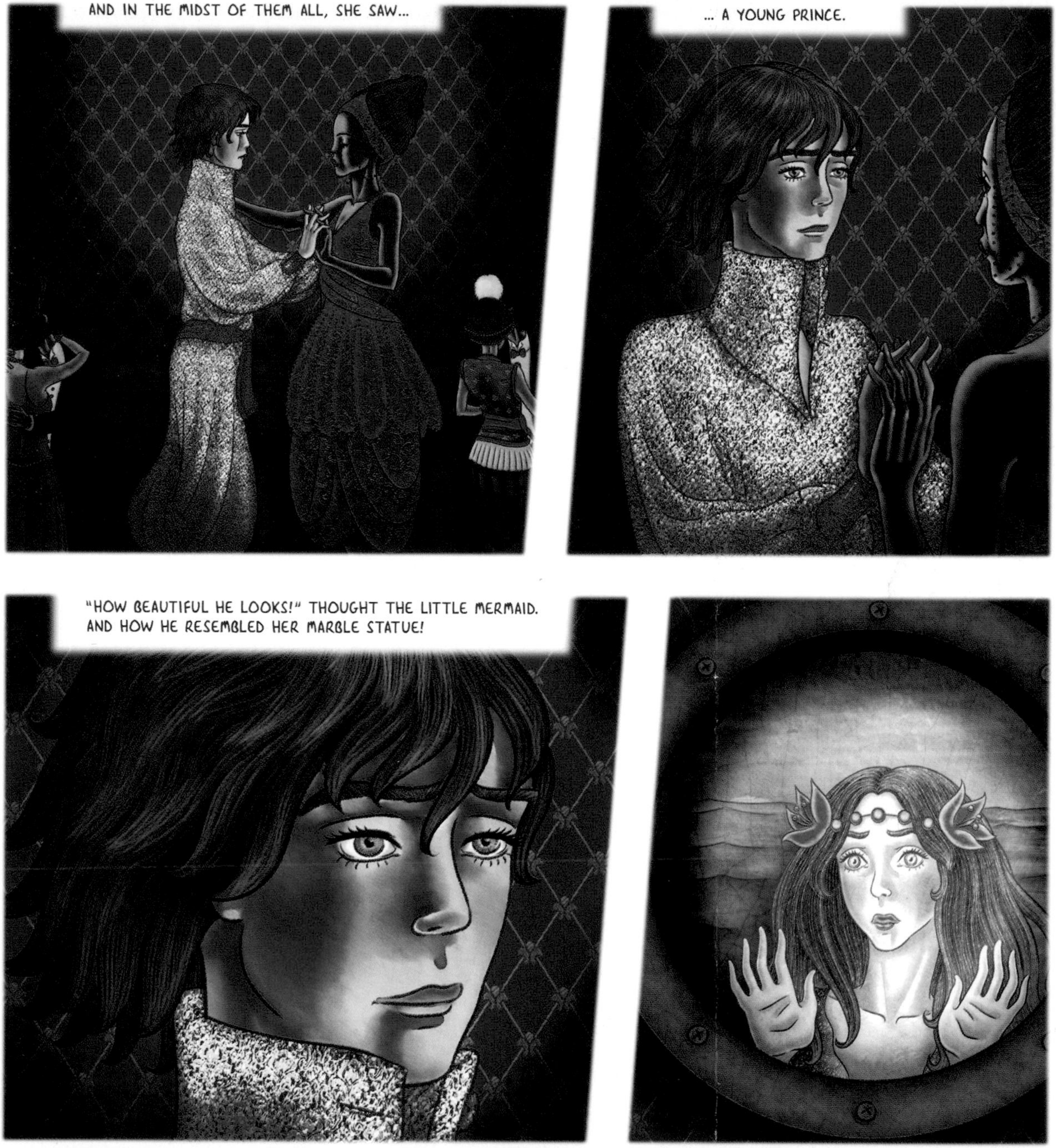
AND IN THE MIDST OF THEM ALL, SHE SAW...
... A YOUNG PRINCE.
"HOW BEAUTIFUL HE LOOKS!" THOUGHT THE LITTLE MERMAID. AND HOW HE RESEMBLED HER MARBLE STATUE!

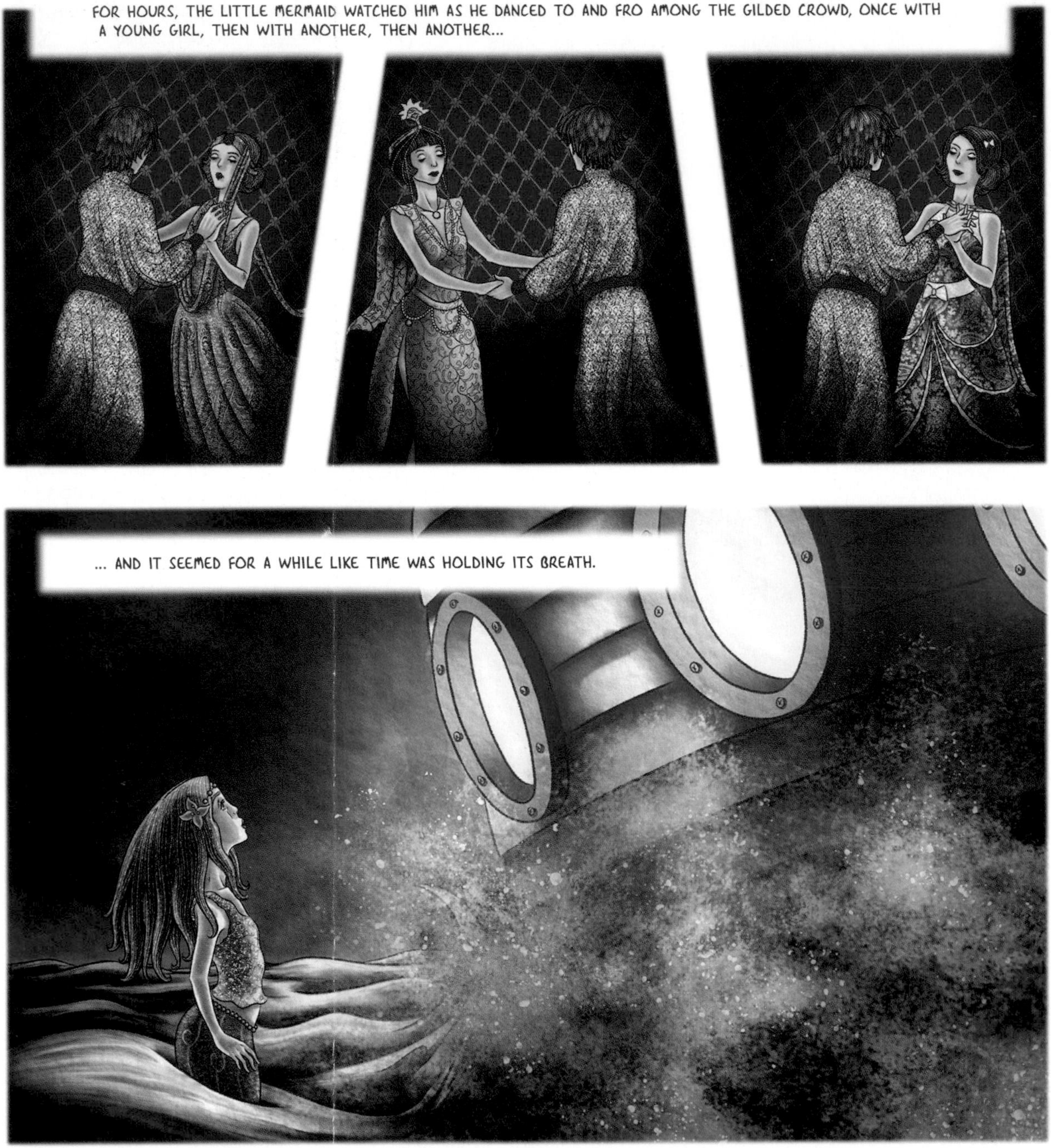
FOR HOURS, THE LITTLE MERMAID WATCHED HIM AS HE DANCED TO AND FRO AMONG THE GILDED CROWD, ONCE WITH A YOUNG GIRL, THEN WITH ANOTHER, THEN ANOTHER...
... AND IT SEEMED FOR A WHILE LIKE TIME WAS HOLDING ITS BREATH.

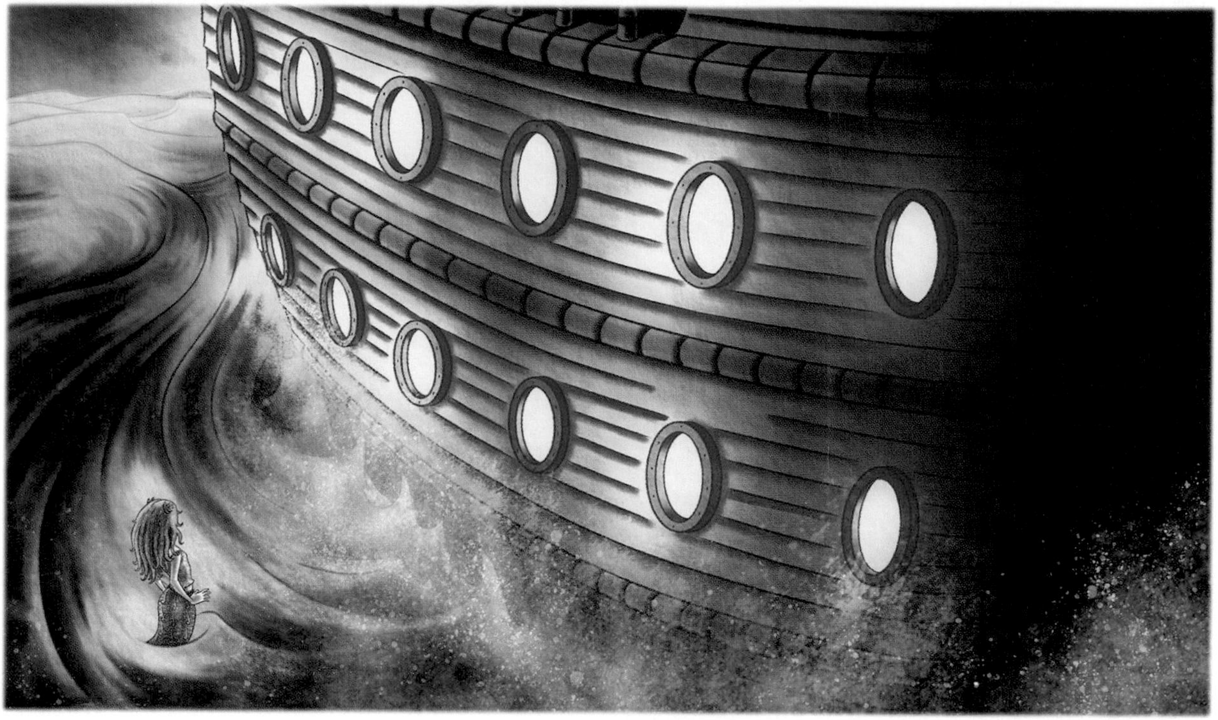

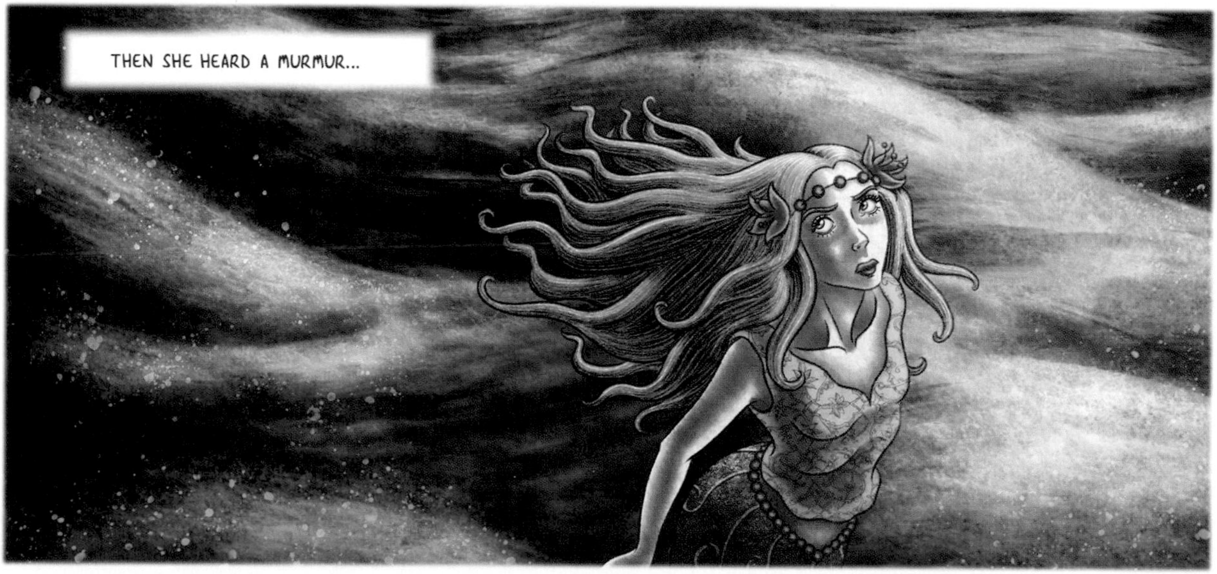
THEN SHE HEARD A MURMUR...

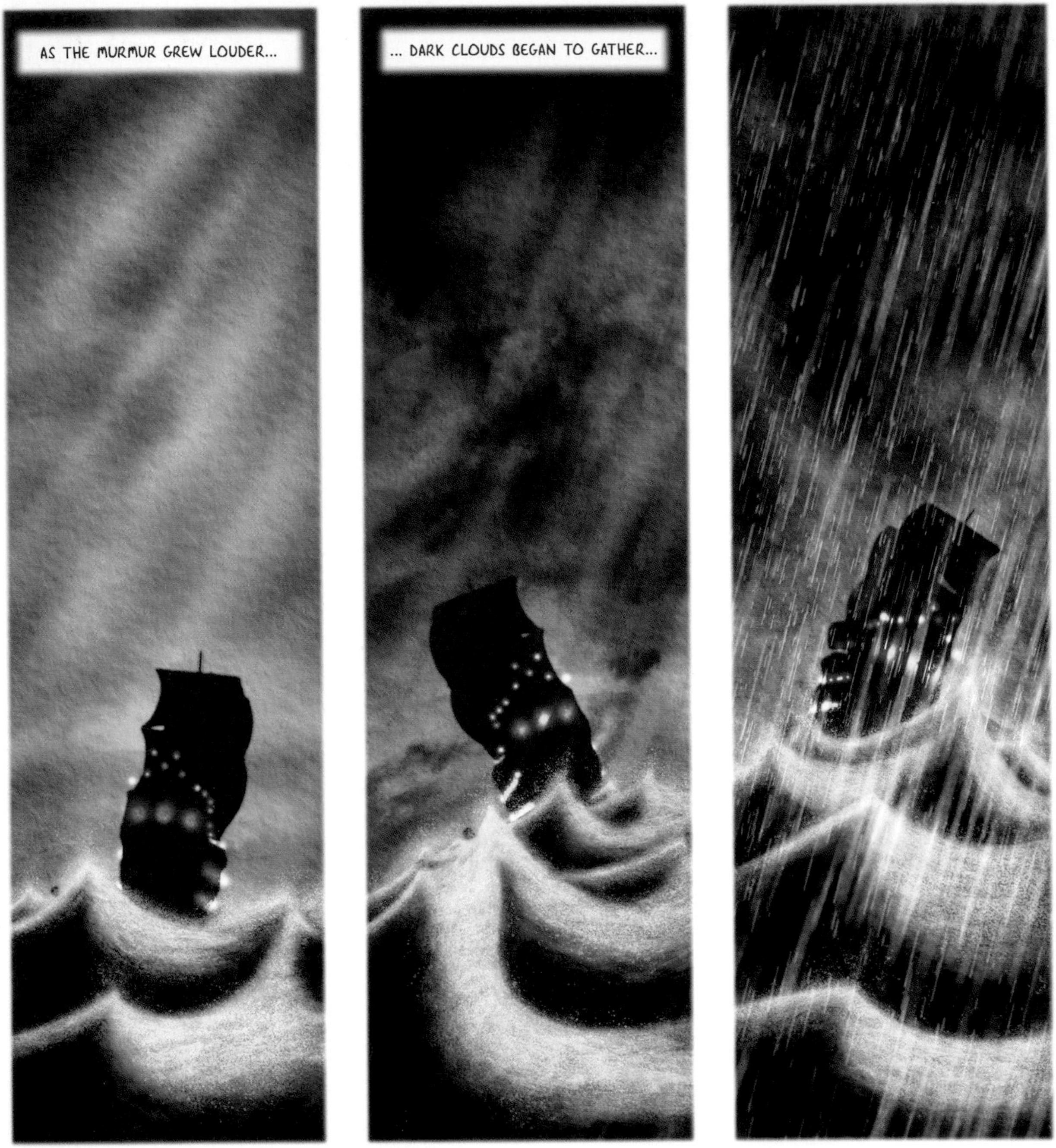
AS THE MURMUR GREW LOUDER...
... DARK CLOUDS BEGAN TO GATHER...

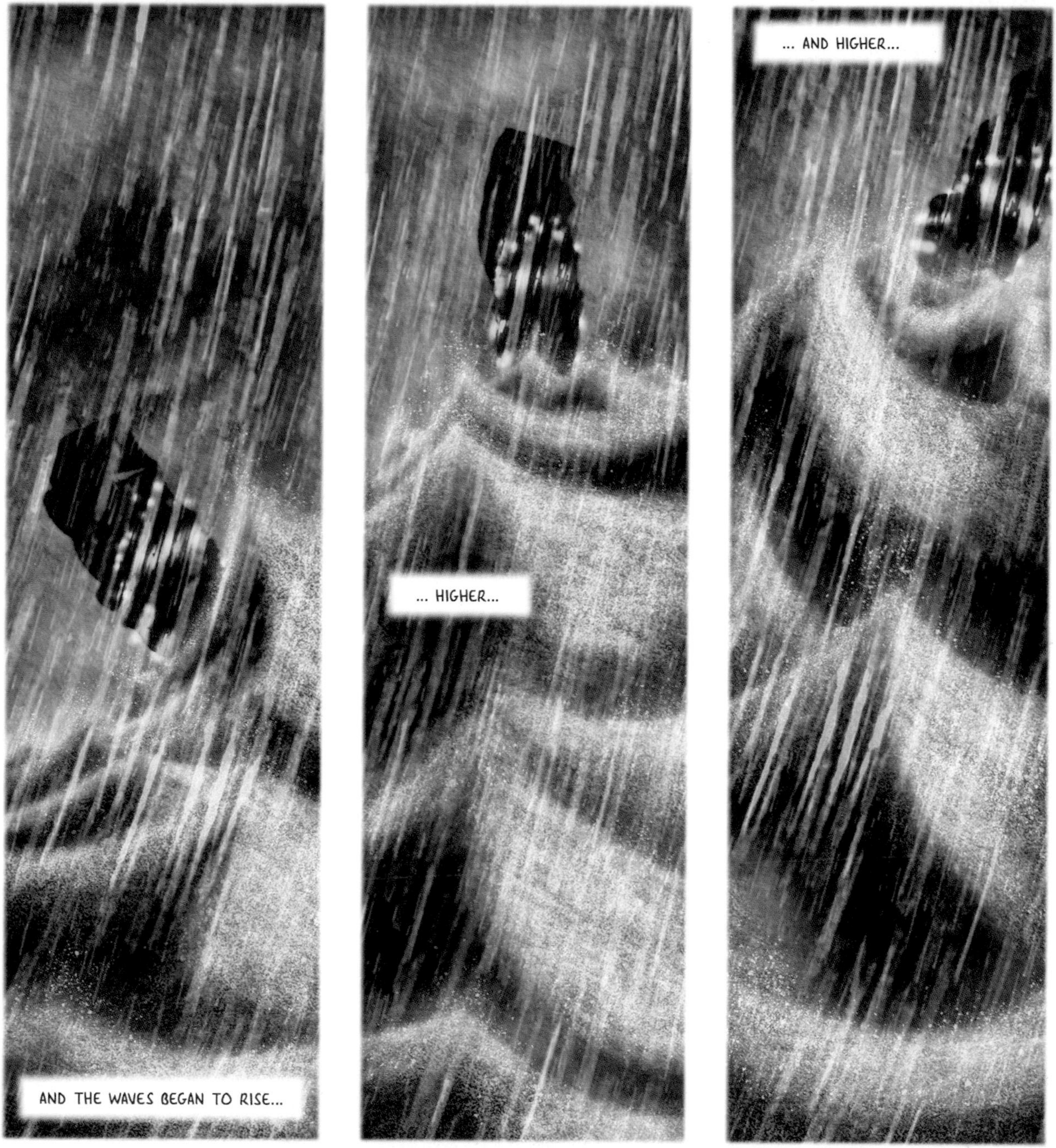
AND THE WAVES BEGAN TO RISE...
... HIGHER...
... AND HIGHER...

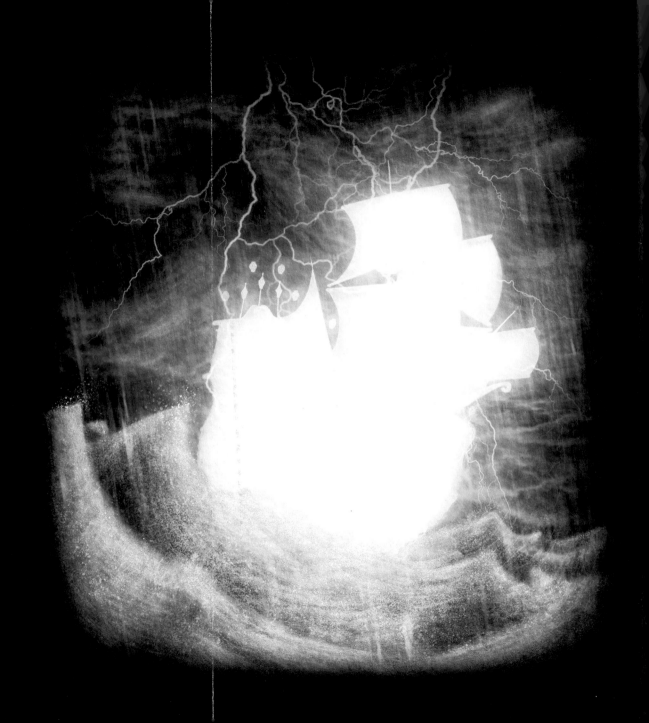

THEN SHE HEARD A DEEP GROAN...

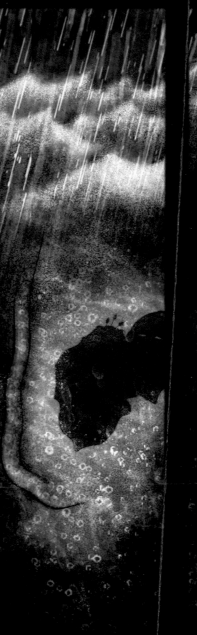

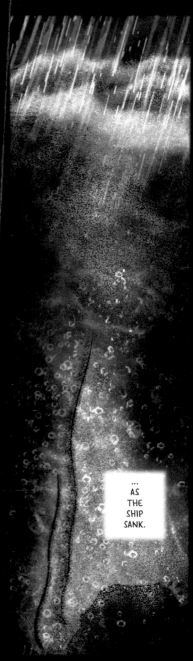

...
AS
THE
SHIP
SANK.

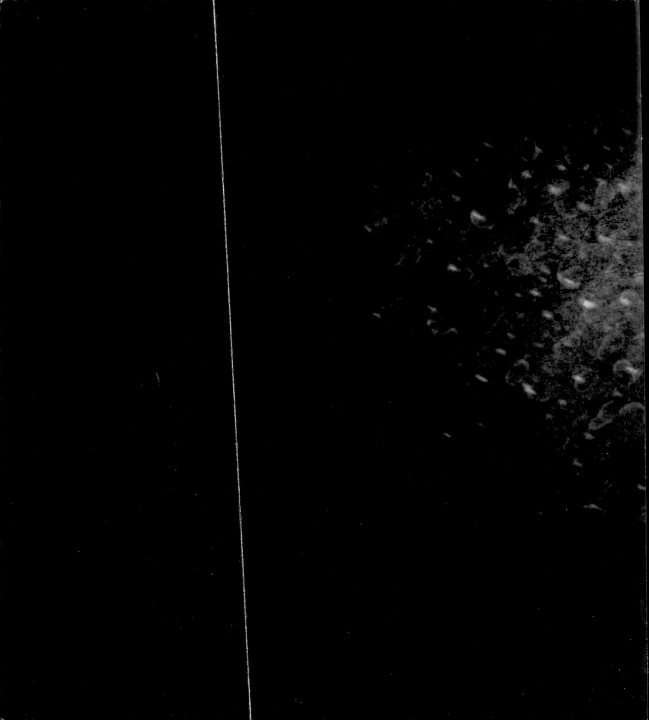

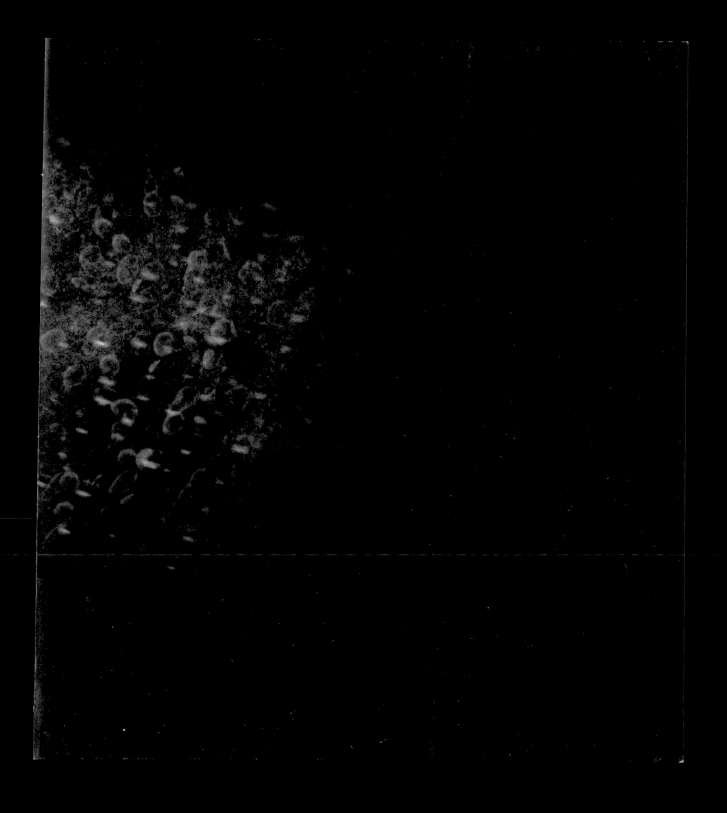

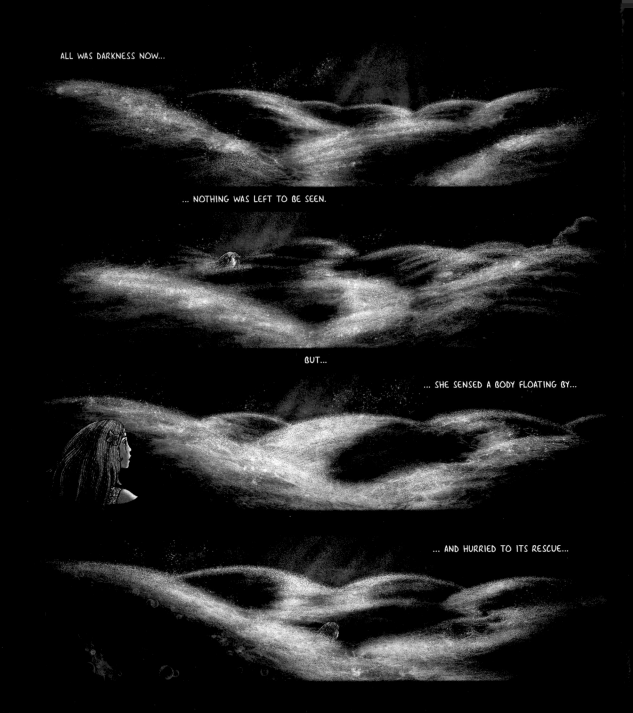

ALL WAS DARKNESS NOW...

... NOTHING WAS LEFT TO BE SEEN.

BUT...

... SHE SENSED A BODY FLOATING BY...

... AND HURRIED TO ITS RESCUE...

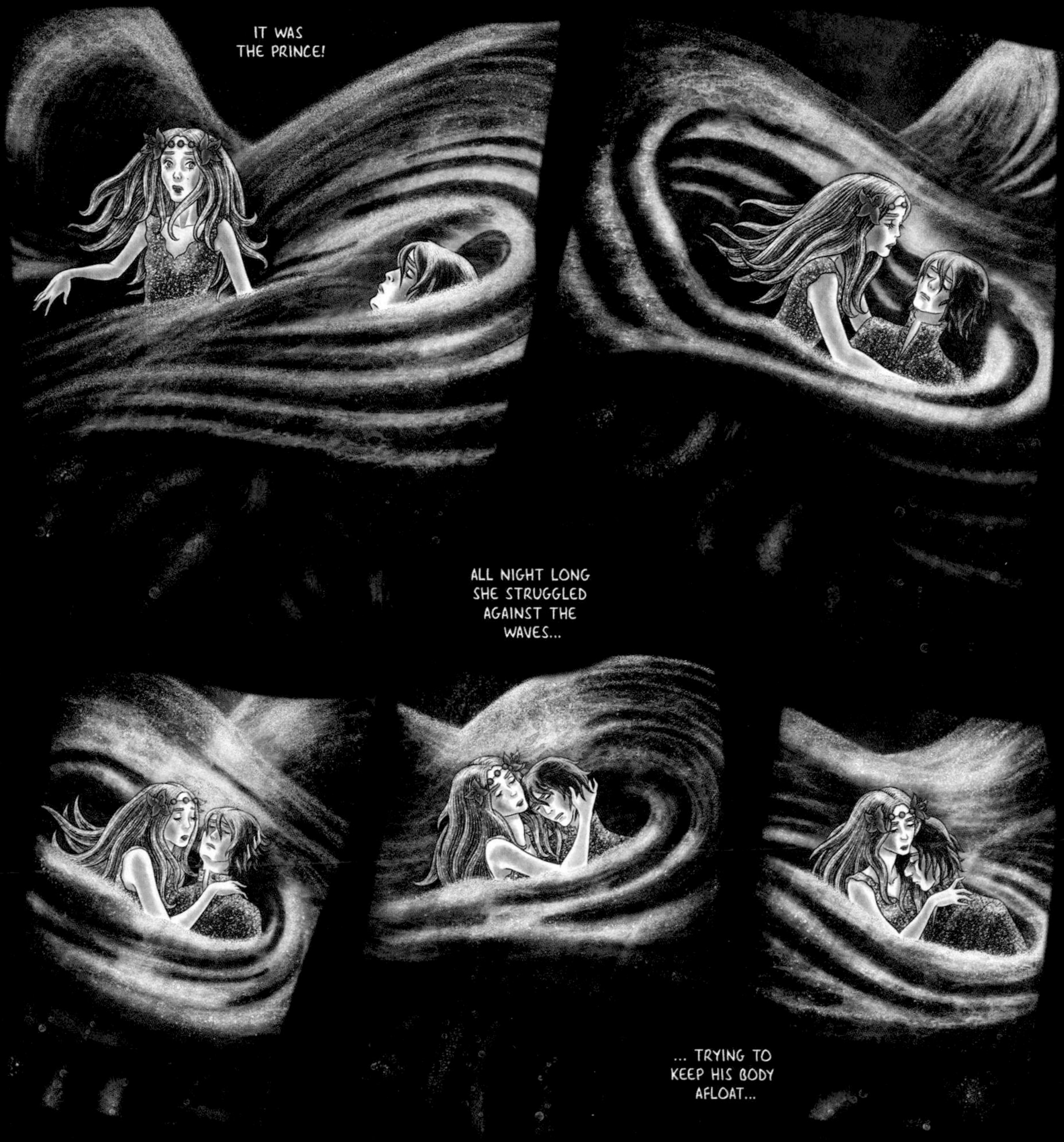
IT WAS
THE PRINCE!
ALL NIGHT LONG
SHE STRUGGLED
AGAINST THE
WAVES...
... TRYING TO
KEEP HIS BODY
AFLOAT...

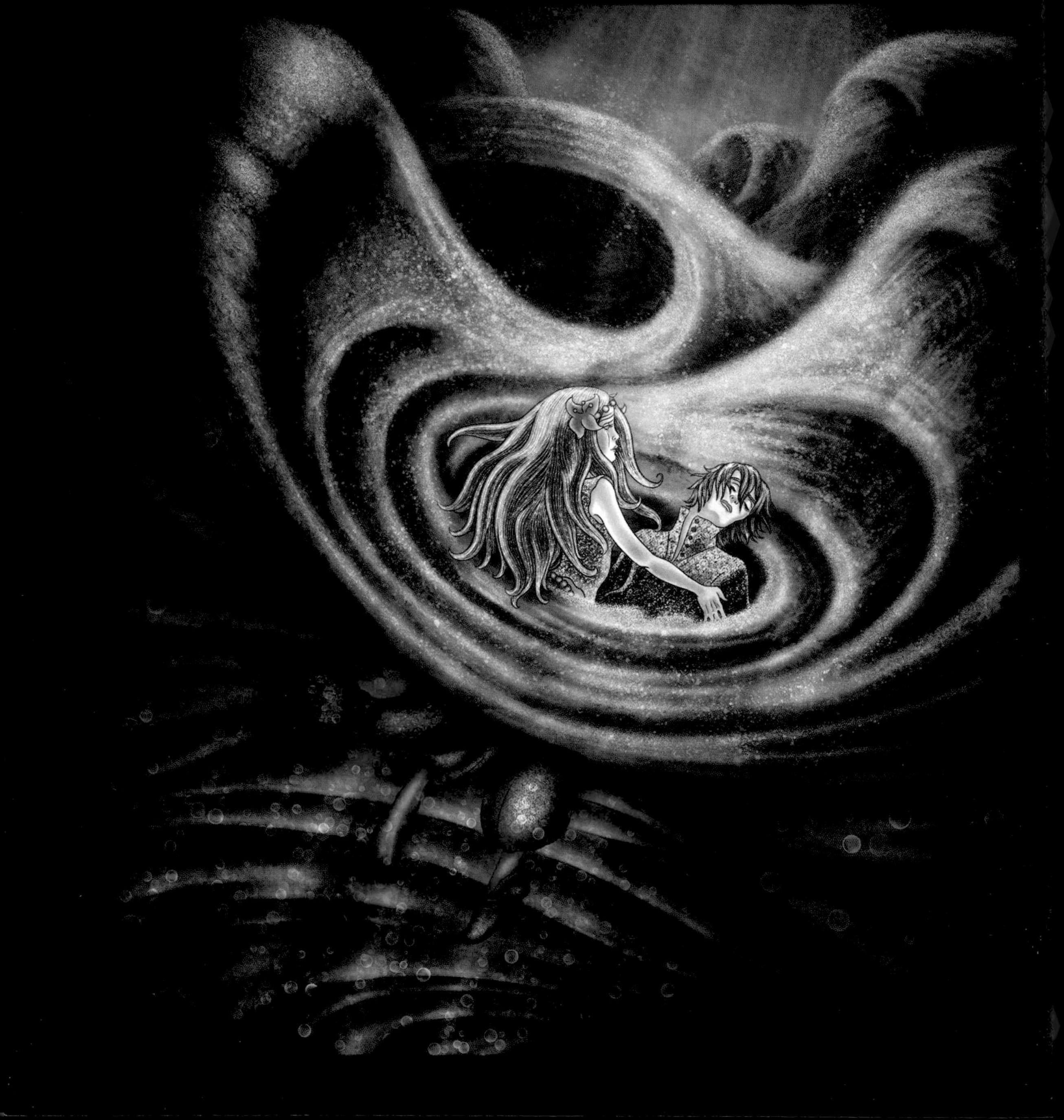

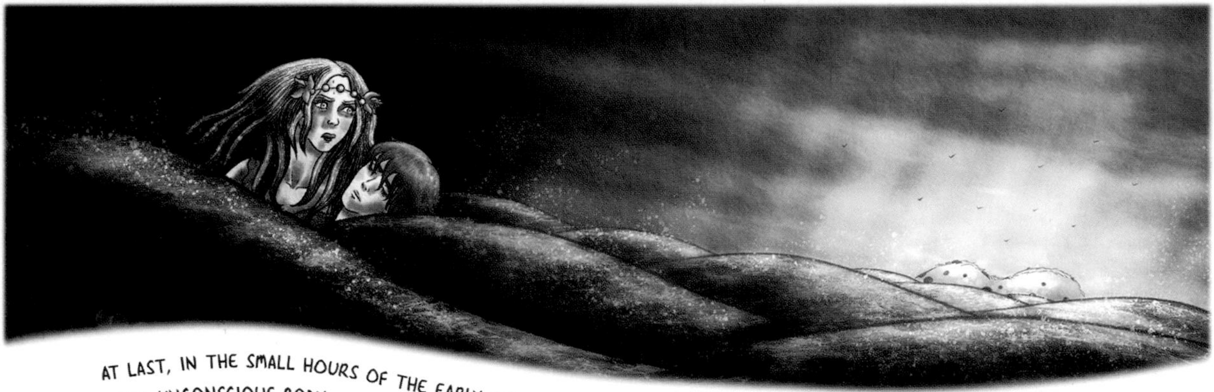

AT LAST, IN THE SMALL HOURS OF THE EARLY MORNING, WHEN SHE FELT SO TIRED SHE COULD BARELY HOLD HIS STILL UNCONSCIOUS BODY...

... SHE SAW LAND IN THE DISTANCE...

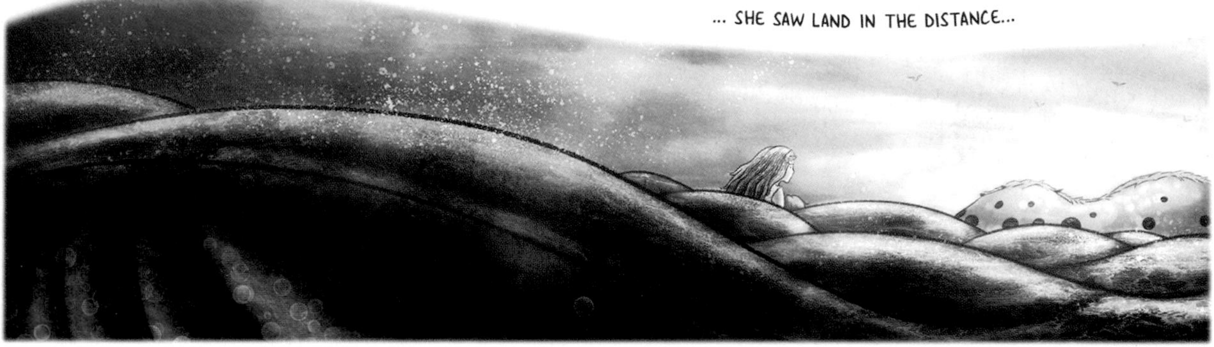

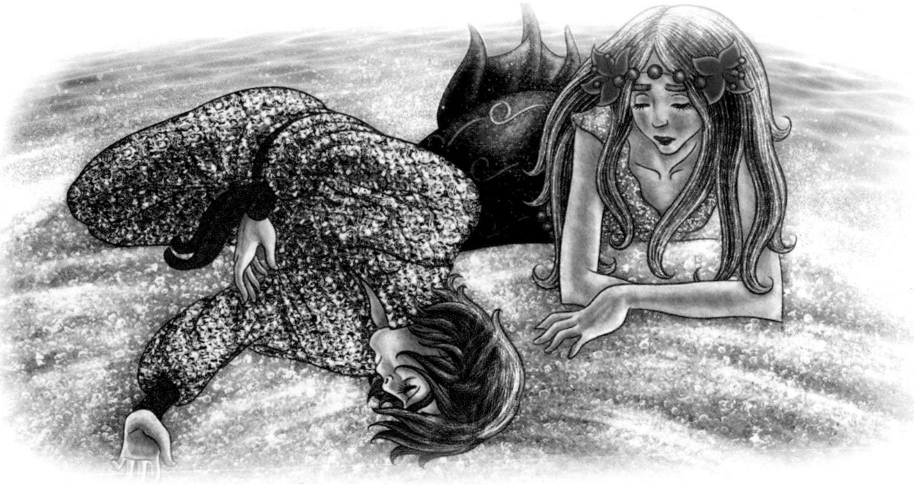

...
AND LAID
THE PRINCE
ON A SANDY
BEACH.

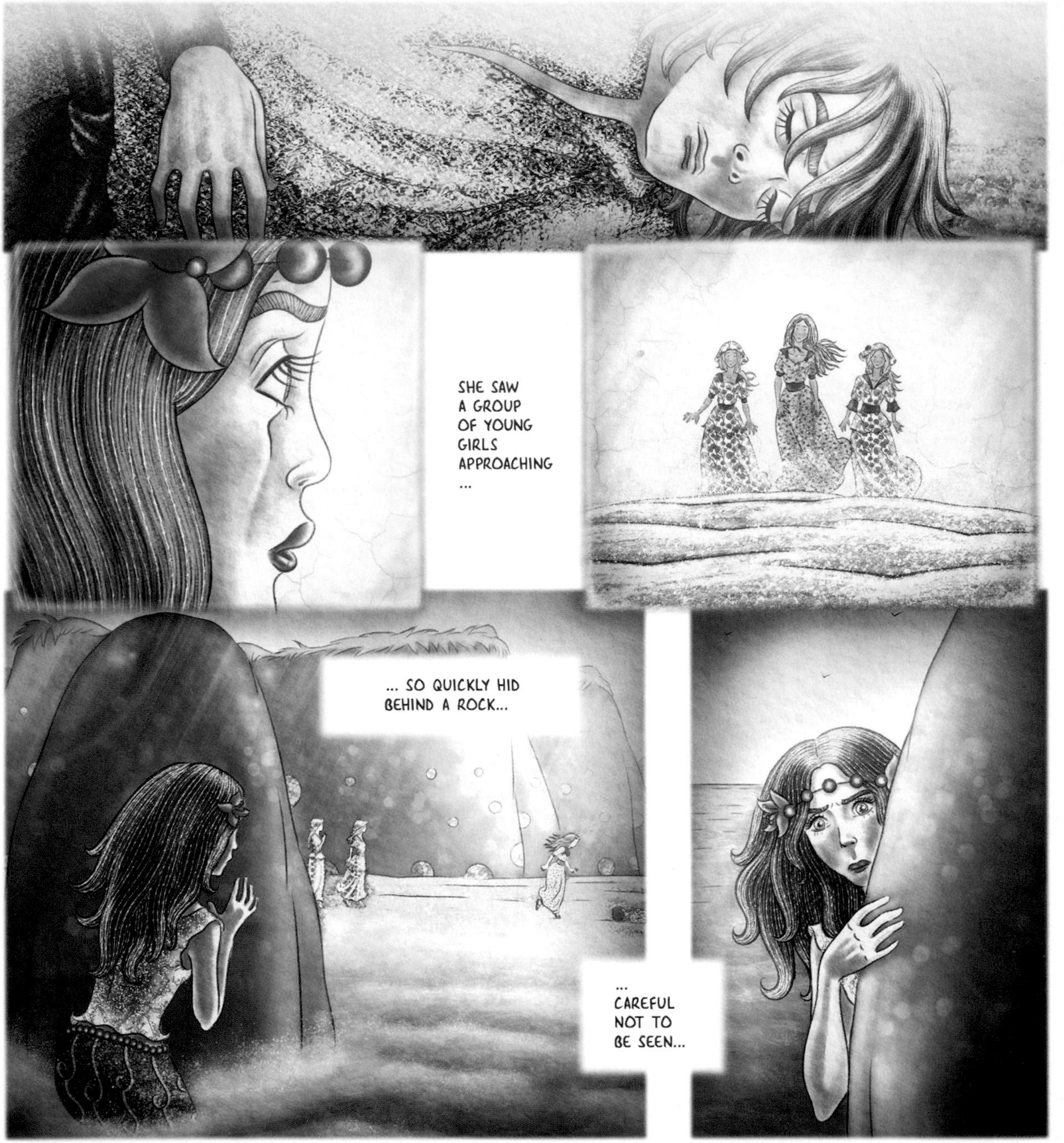
SHE SAW A GROUP OF YOUNG GIRLS APPROACHING ...
... SO QUICKLY HID BEHIND A ROCK...
... CAREFUL NOT TO BE SEEN...

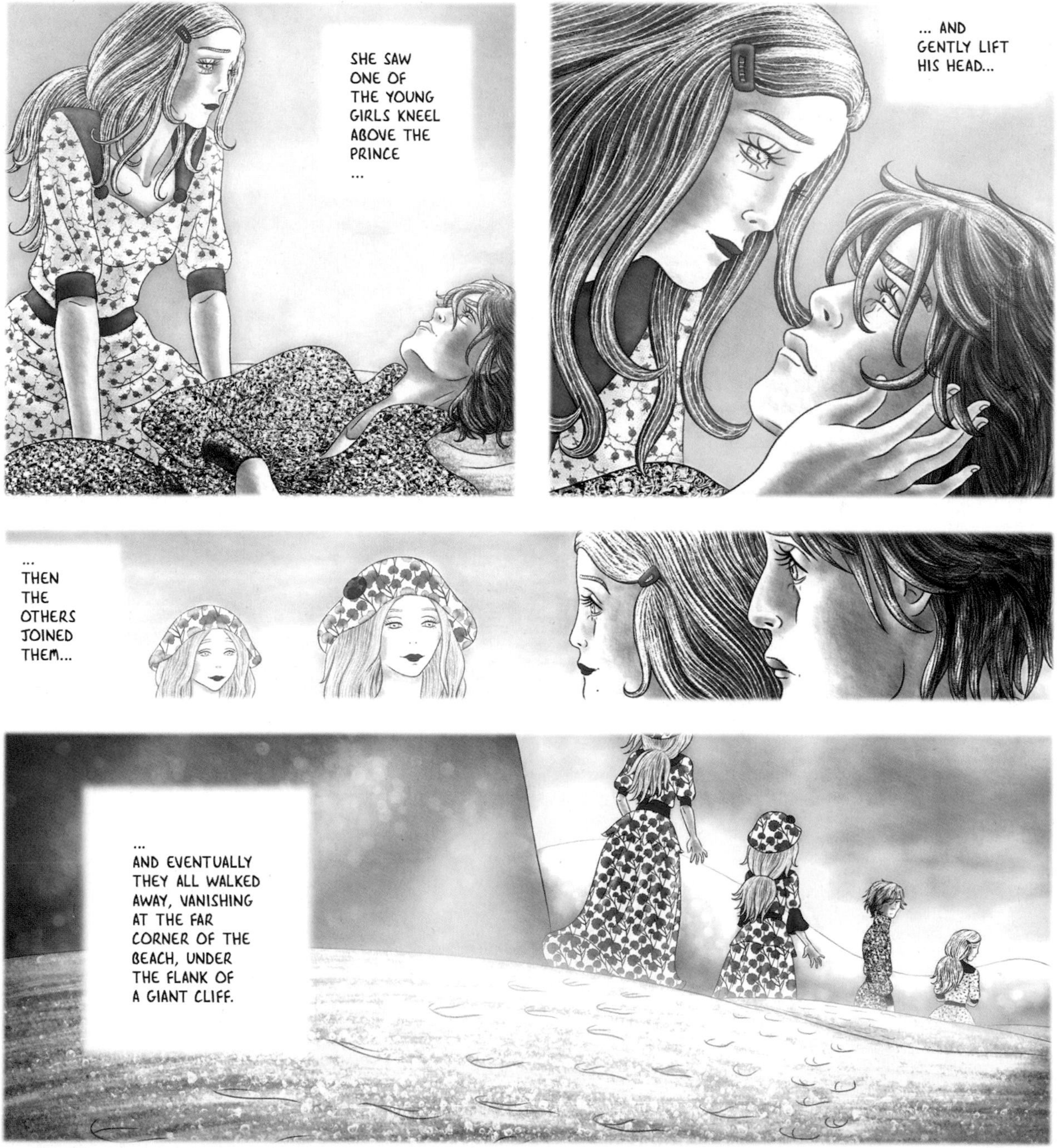
SHE SAW ONE OF THE YOUNG GIRLS KNEEL ABOVE THE PRINCE ...
... AND GENTLY LIFT HIS HEAD...
... THEN THE OTHERS JOINED THEM...
... AND EVENTUALLY THEY ALL WALKED AWAY, VANISHING AT THE FAR CORNER OF THE BEACH, UNDER THE FLANK OF A GIANT CLIFF.

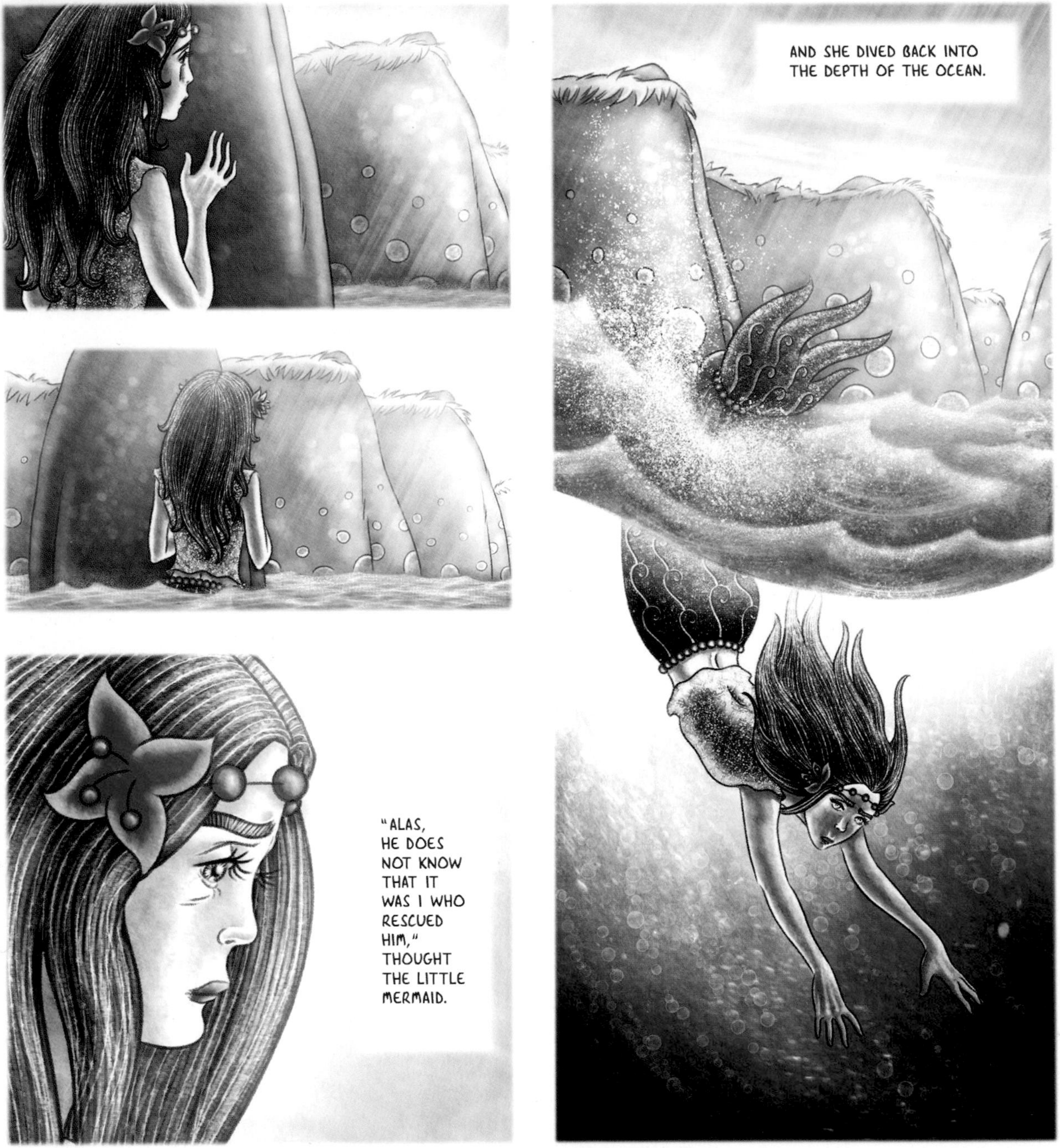
"ALAS, HE DOES NOT KNOW THAT IT WAS I WHO RESCUED HIM," THOUGHT THE LITTLE MERMAID.
AND SHE DIVED BACK INTO THE DEPTH OF THE OCEAN.

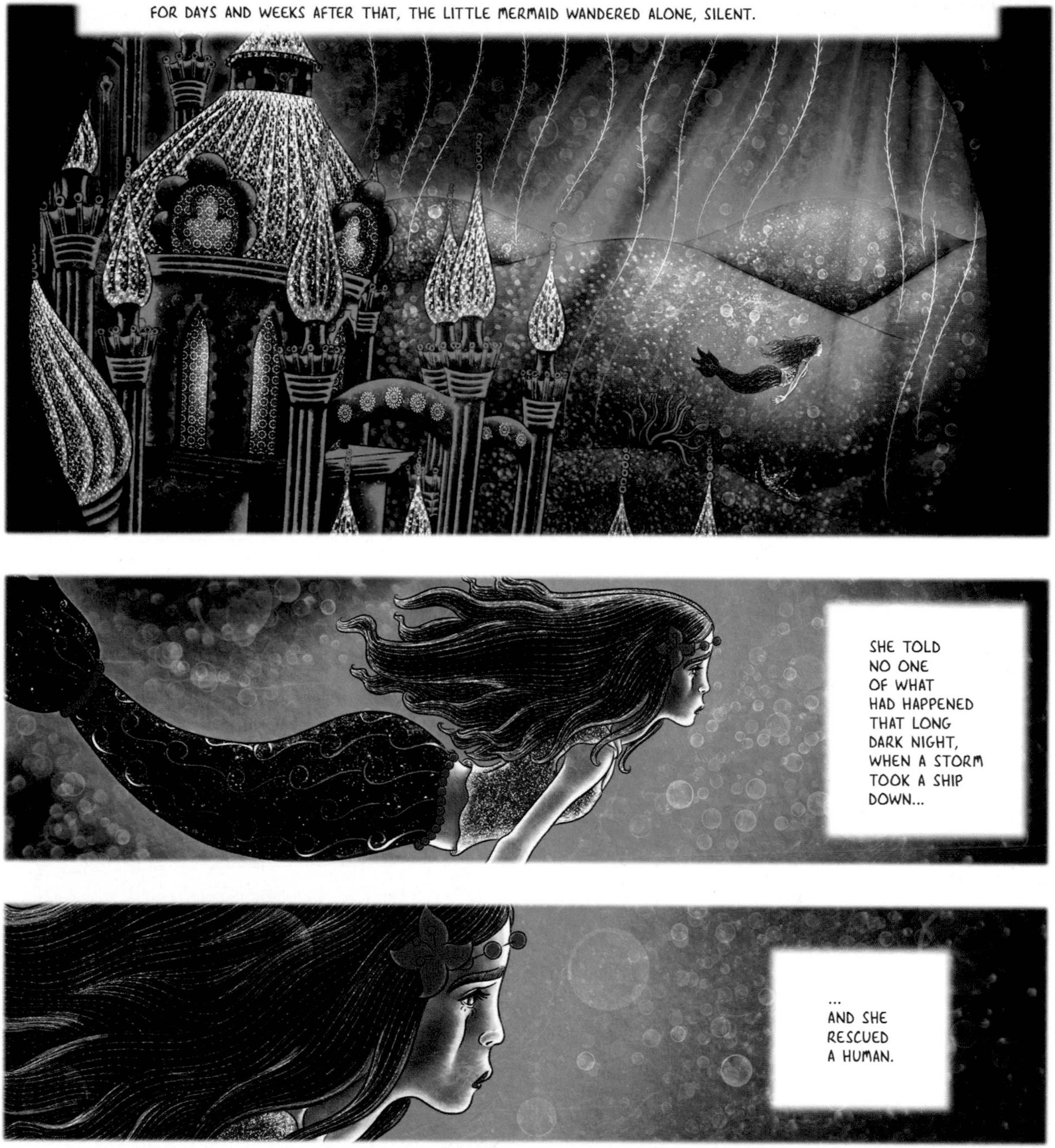
FOR DAYS AND WEEKS AFTER THAT, THE LITTLE MERMAID WANDERED ALONE, SILENT.
SHE TOLD NO ONE OF WHAT HAD HAPPENED THAT LONG DARK NIGHT, WHEN A STORM TOOK A SHIP DOWN...
... AND SHE RESCUED A HUMAN.

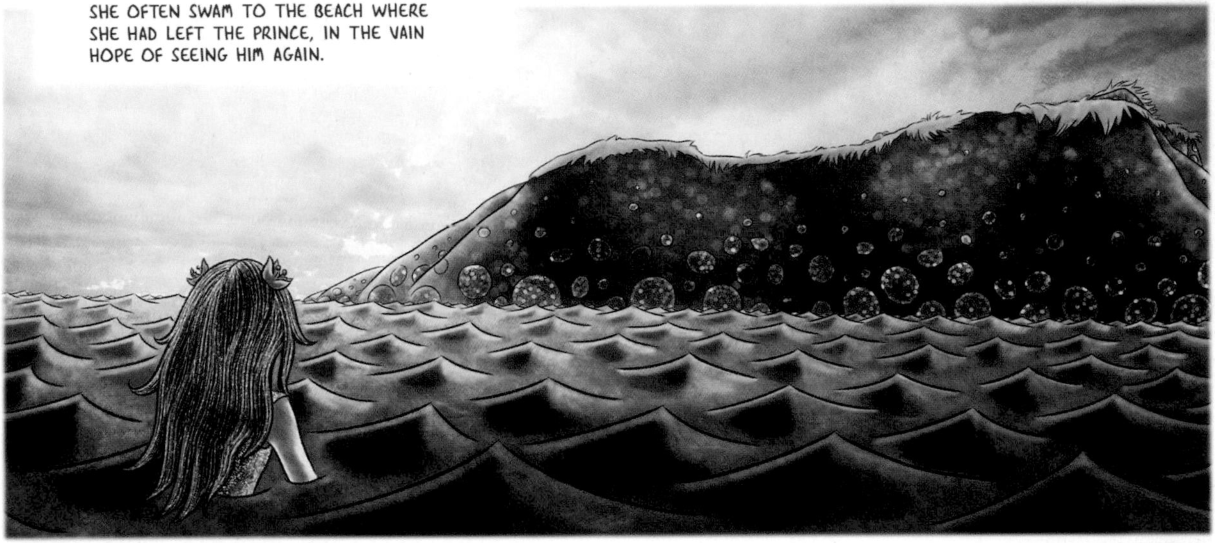
SHE OFTEN SWAM TO THE BEACH WHERE SHE HAD LEFT THE PRINCE, IN THE VAIN HOPE OF SEEING HIM AGAIN.

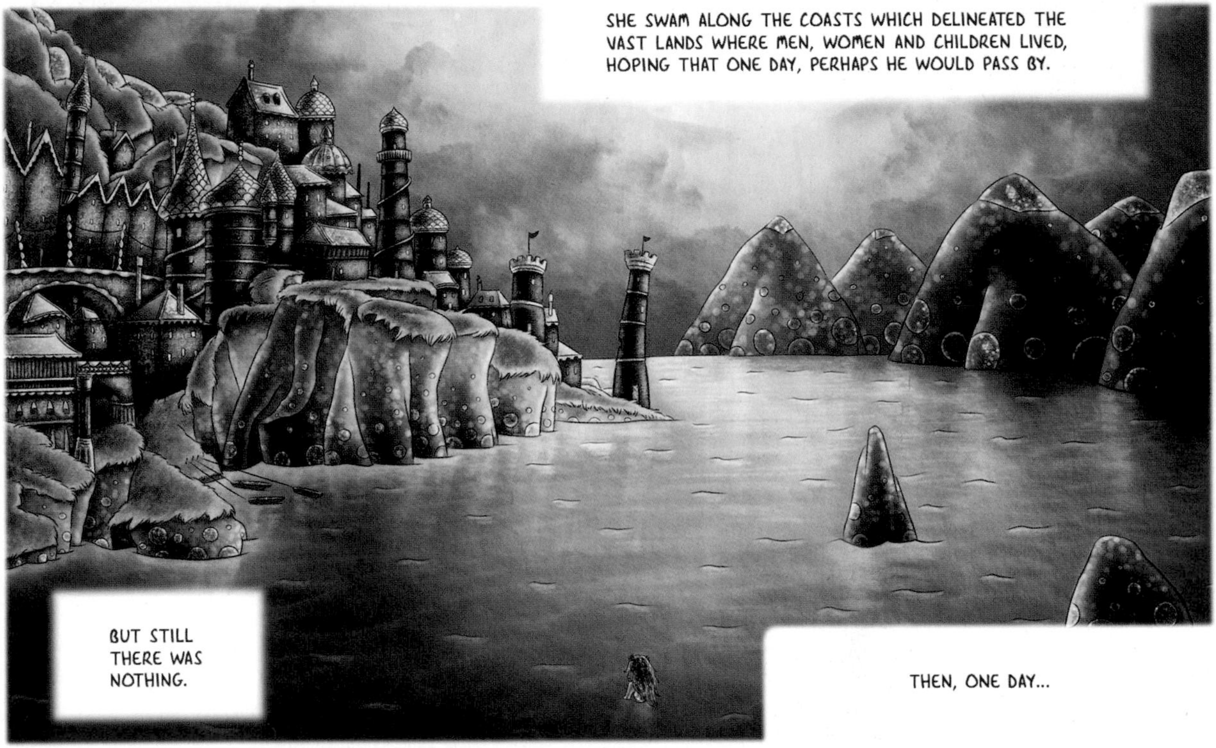
SHE SWAM ALONG THE COASTS WHICH DELINEATED THE VAST LANDS WHERE MEN, WOMEN AND CHILDREN LIVED, HOPING THAT ONE DAY, PERHAPS HE WOULD PASS BY.
BUT STILL THERE WAS NOTHING.
THEN, ONE DAY...

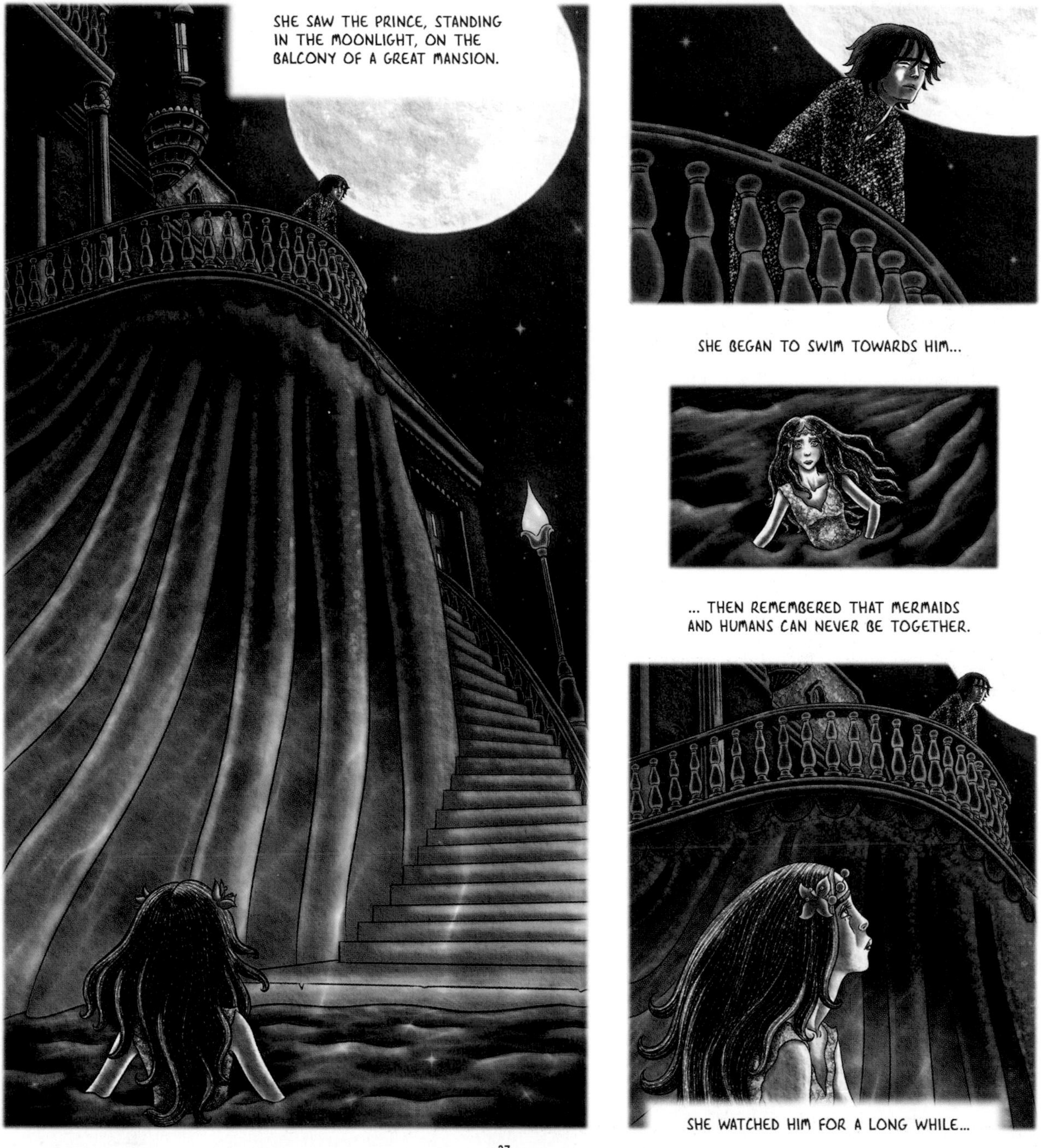
SHE SAW THE PRINCE, STANDING IN THE MOONLIGHT, ON THE BALCONY OF A GREAT MANSION.
SHE BEGAN TO SWIM TOWARDS HIM...
... THEN REMEMBERED THAT MERMAIDS AND HUMANS CAN NEVER BE TOGETHER.
SHE WATCHED HIM FOR A LONG WHILE...

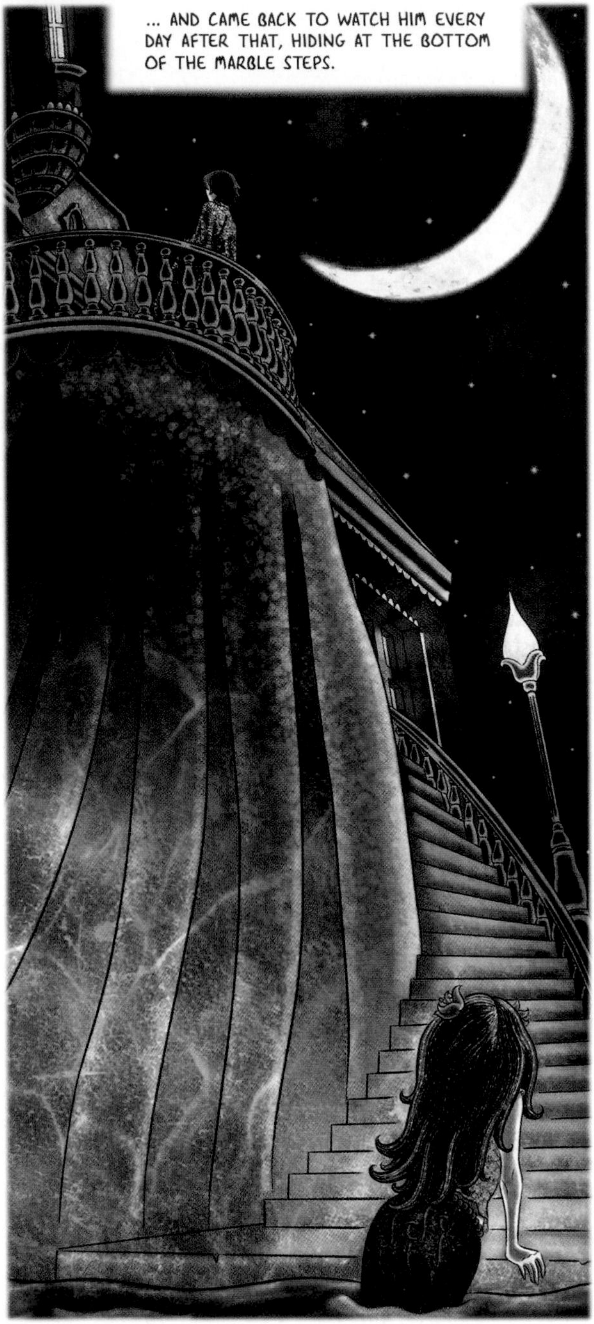
... AND CAME BACK TO WATCH HIM EVERY DAY AFTER THAT, HIDING AT THE BOTTOM OF THE MARBLE STEPS.

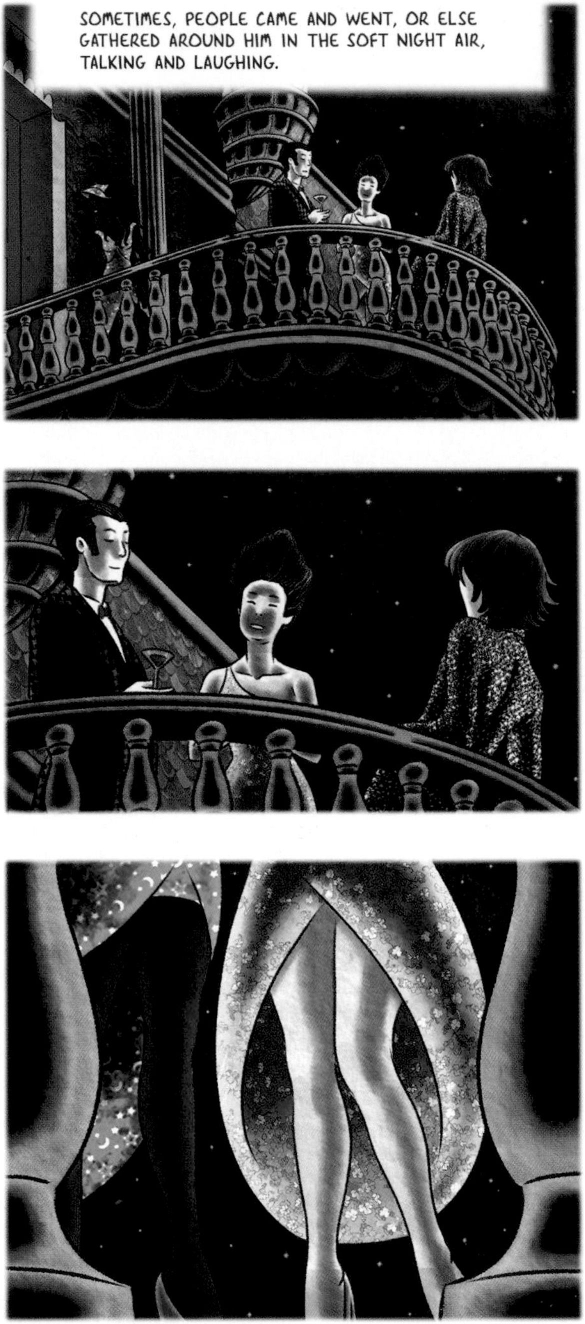
SOMETIMES, PEOPLE CAME AND WENT, OR ELSE GATHERED AROUND HIM IN THE SOFT NIGHT AIR, TALKING AND LAUGHING.

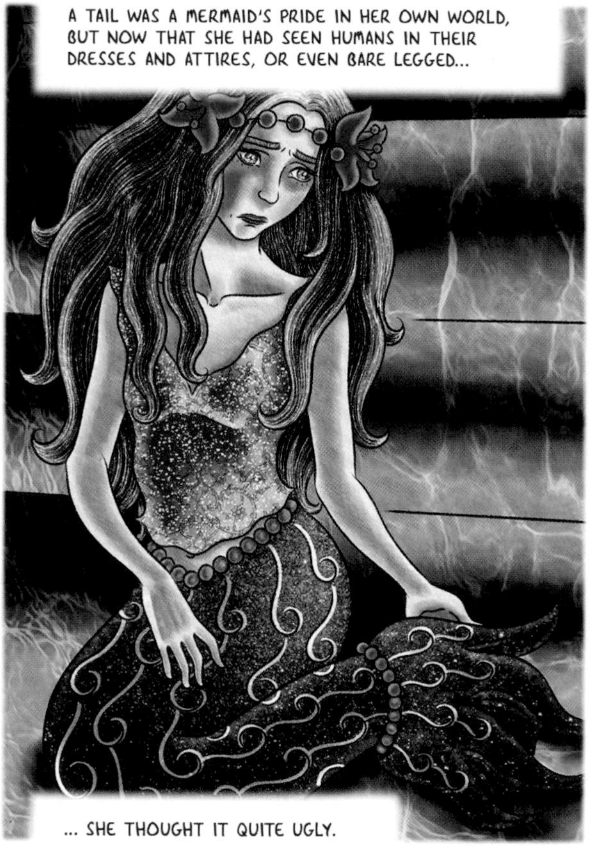
A TAIL WAS A MERMAID'S PRIDE IN HER OWN WORLD, BUT NOW THAT SHE HAD SEEN HUMANS IN THEIR DRESSES AND ATTIRES, OR EVEN BARE LEGGED...
... SHE THOUGHT IT QUITE UGLY.

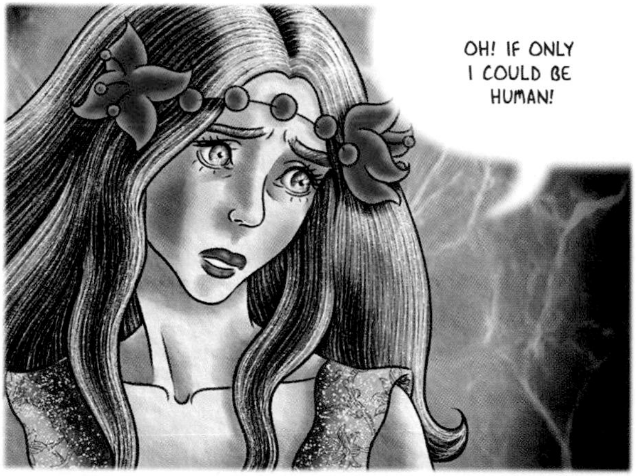
OH! IF ONLY I COULD BE HUMAN!

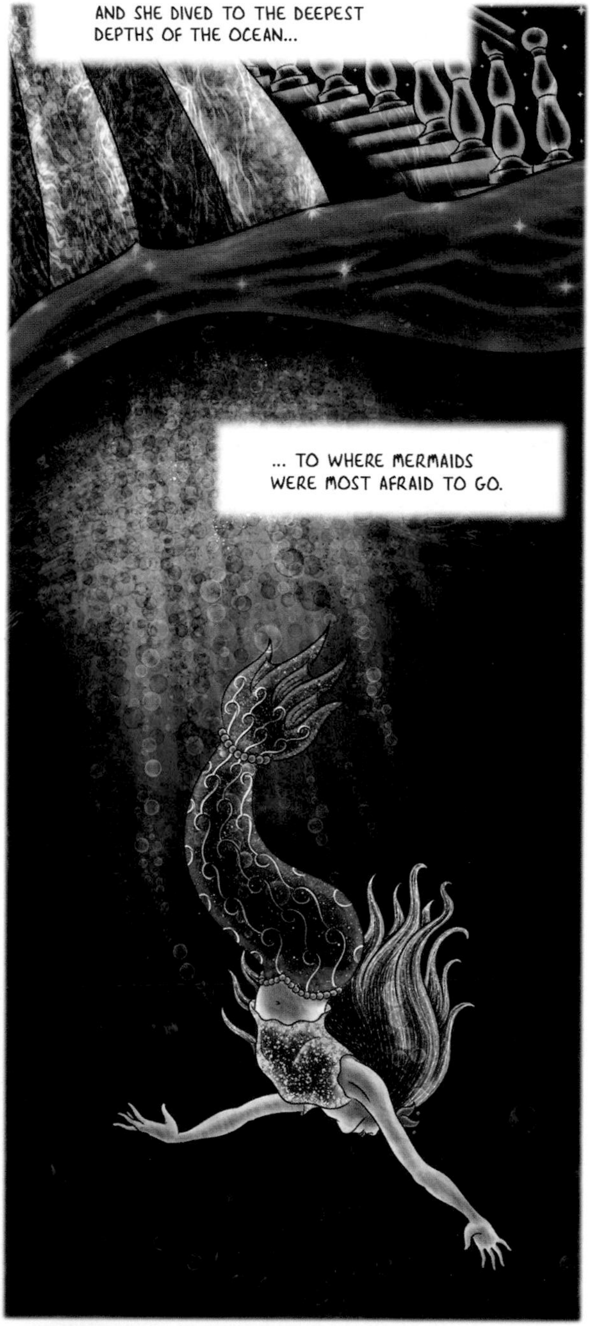
AND SHE DIVED TO THE DEEPEST DEPTHS OF THE OCEAN...
... TO WHERE MERMAIDS WERE MOST AFRAID TO GO.

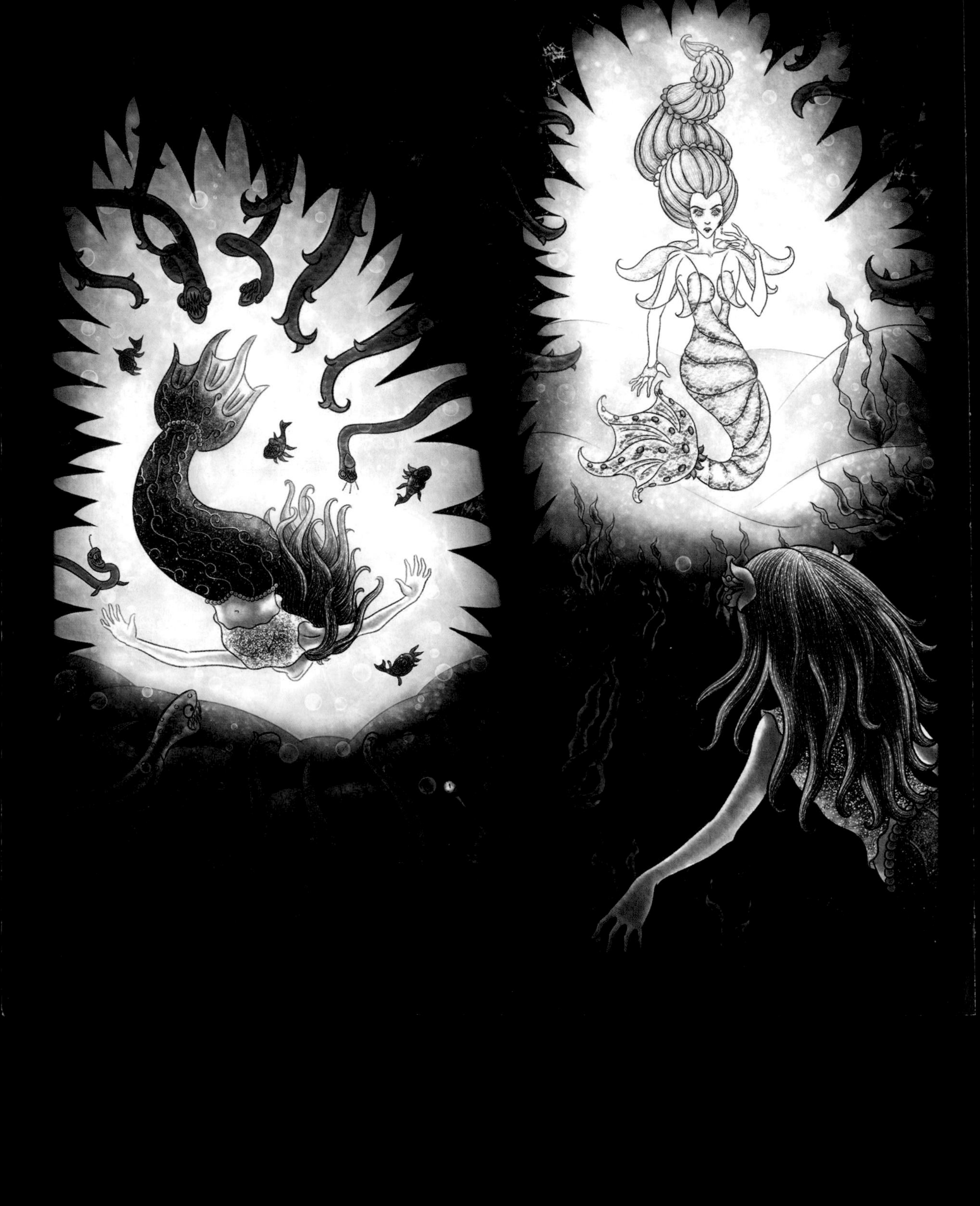

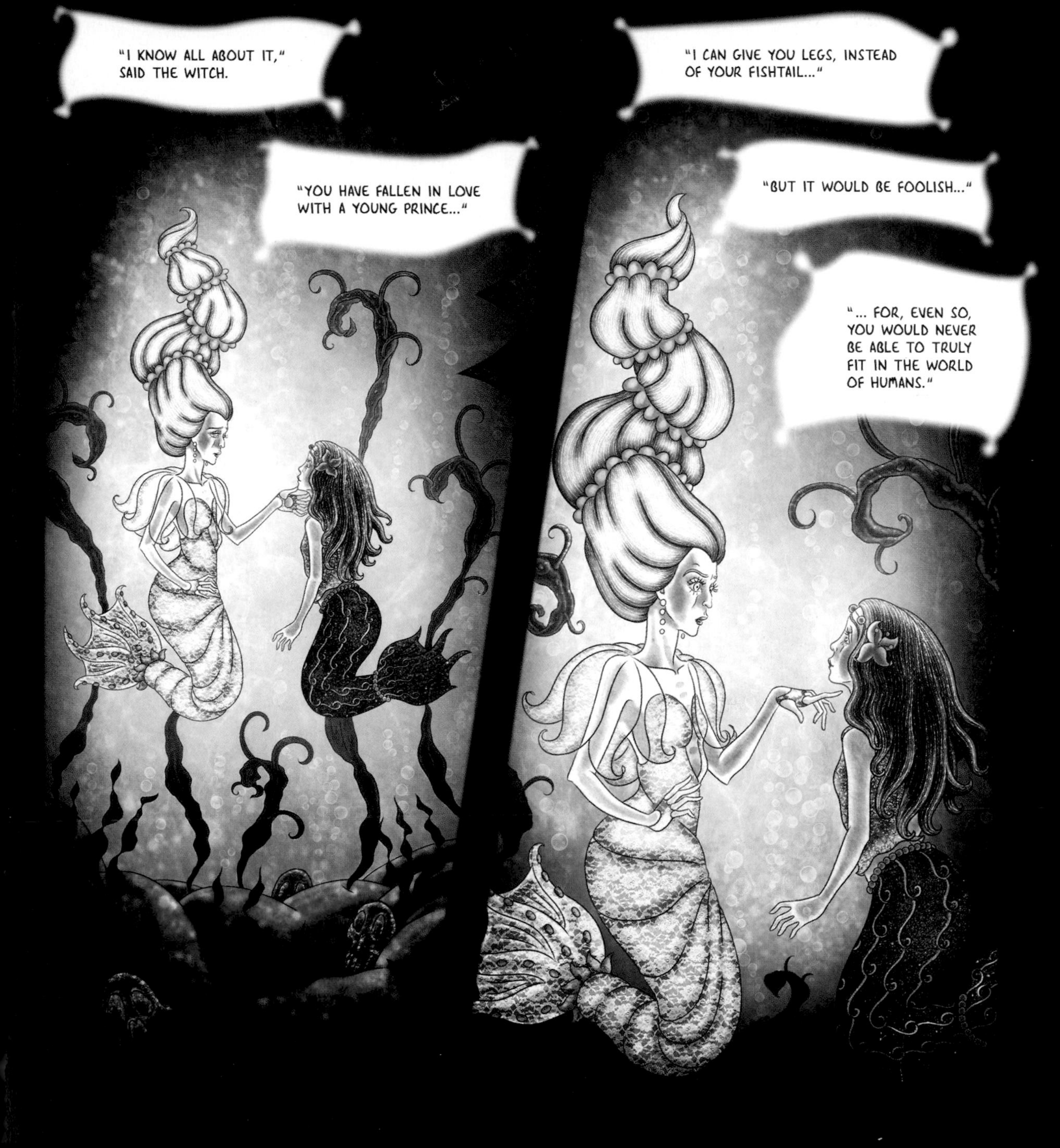
"I KNOW ALL ABOUT IT," SAID THE WITCH.
"YOU HAVE FALLEN IN LOVE WITH A YOUNG PRINCE..."
"I CAN GIVE YOU LEGS, INSTEAD OF YOUR FISHTAIL..."
"BUT IT WOULD BE FOOLISH..."
"... FOR, EVEN SO, YOU WOULD NEVER BE ABLE TO TRULY FIT IN THE WORLD OF HUMANS."

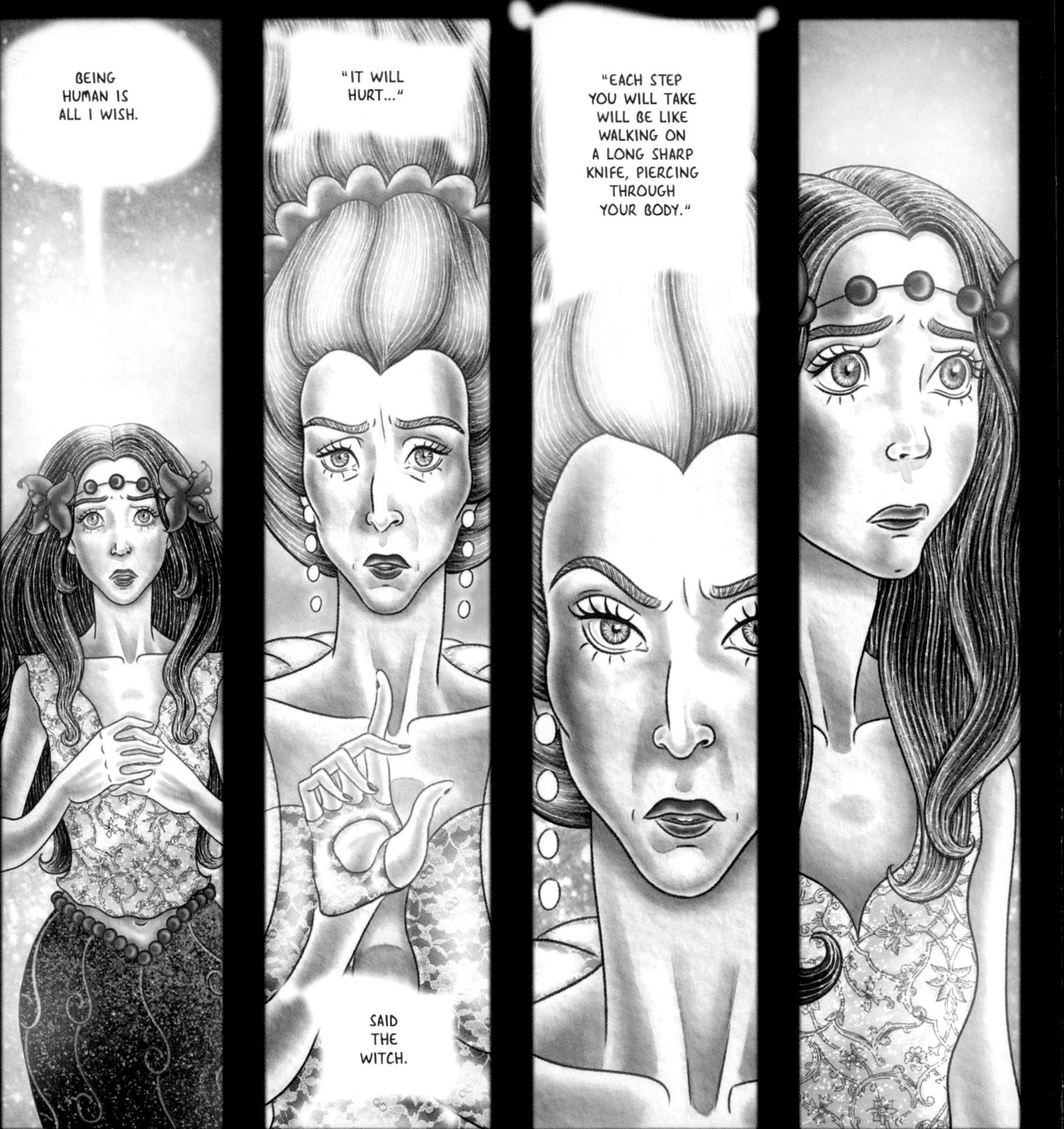
BEING HUMAN IS ALL I WISH.
"IT WILL HURT..."
SAID THE WITCH.
"EACH STEP YOU WILL TAKE WILL BE LIKE WALKING ON A LONG SHARP KNIFE, PIERCING THROUGH YOUR BODY."

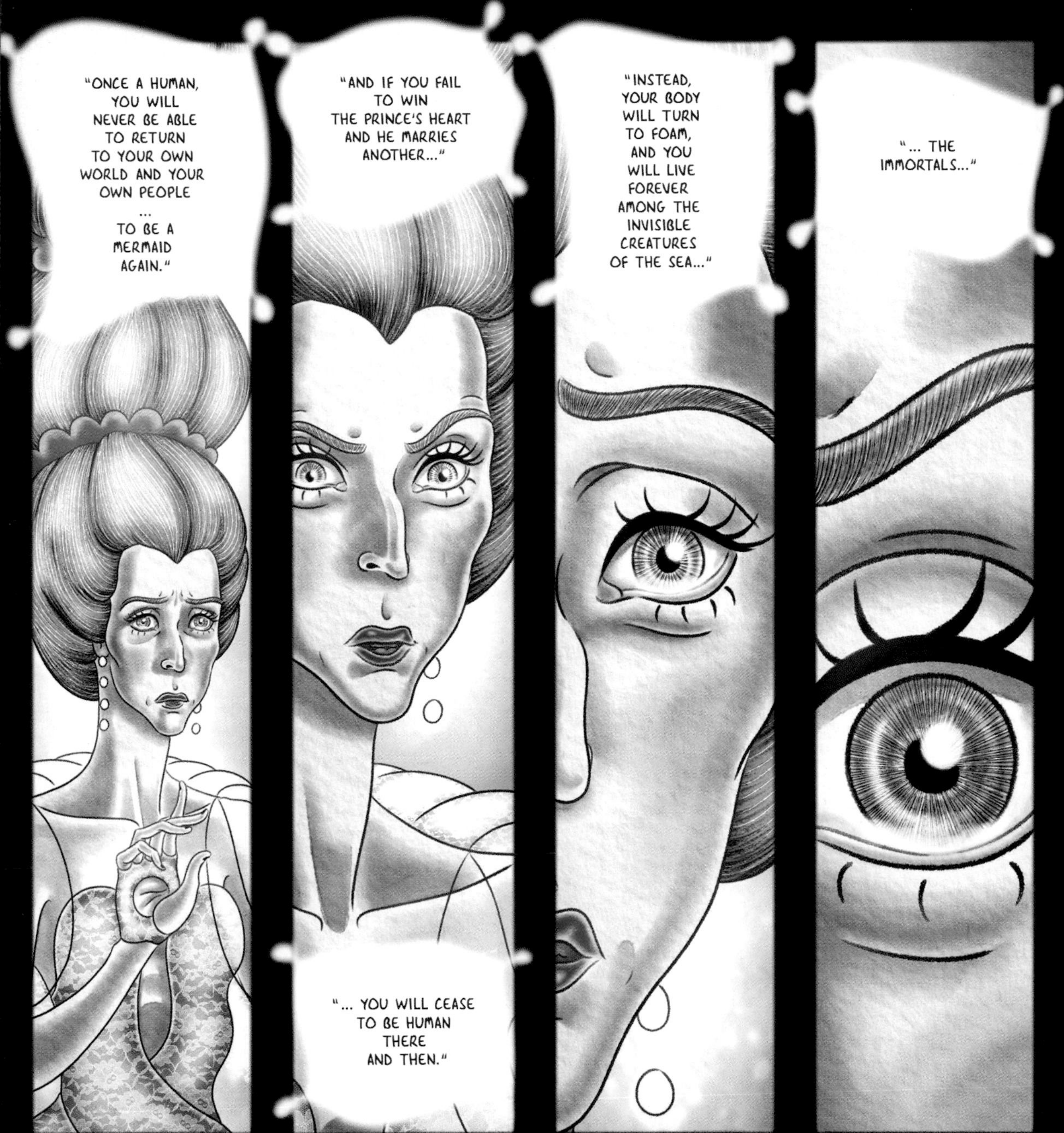
"ONCE A HUMAN, YOU WILL NEVER BE ABLE TO RETURN TO YOUR OWN WORLD AND YOUR OWN PEOPLE ... TO BE A MERMAID AGAIN."
"AND IF YOU FAIL TO WIN THE PRINCE'S HEART AND HE MARRIES ANOTHER..."
"... YOU WILL CEASE TO BE HUMAN THERE AND THEN."
"INSTEAD, YOUR BODY WILL TURN TO FOAM, AND YOU WILL LIVE FOREVER AMONG THE INVISIBLE CREATURES OF THE SEA..."
"... THE IMMORTALS..."

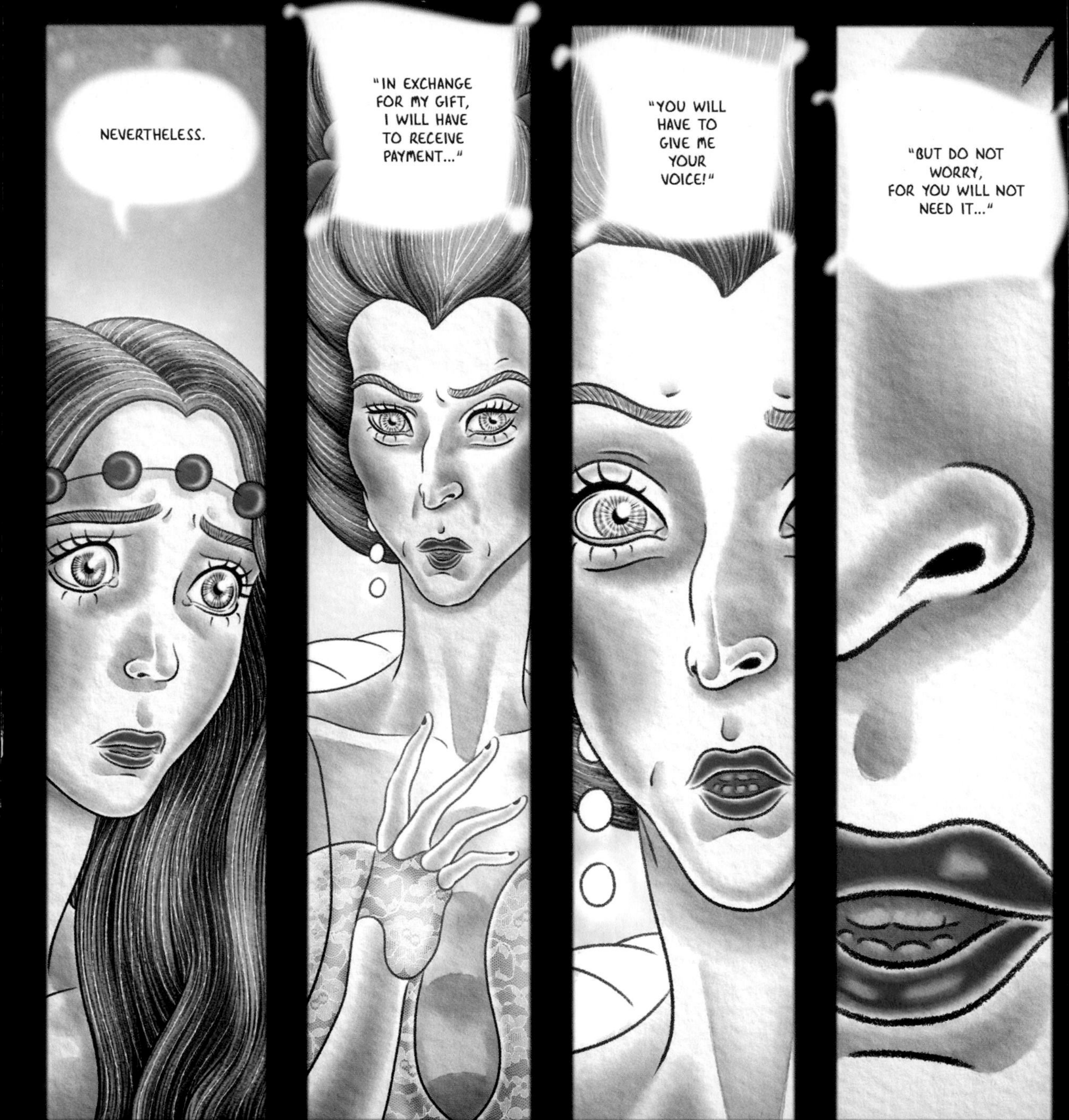
NEVERTHELESS.
"IN EXCHANGE FOR MY GIFT, I WILL HAVE TO RECEIVE PAYMENT..."
"YOU WILL HAVE TO GIVE ME YOUR VOICE!"
"BUT DO NOT WORRY, FOR YOU WILL NOT NEED IT..."

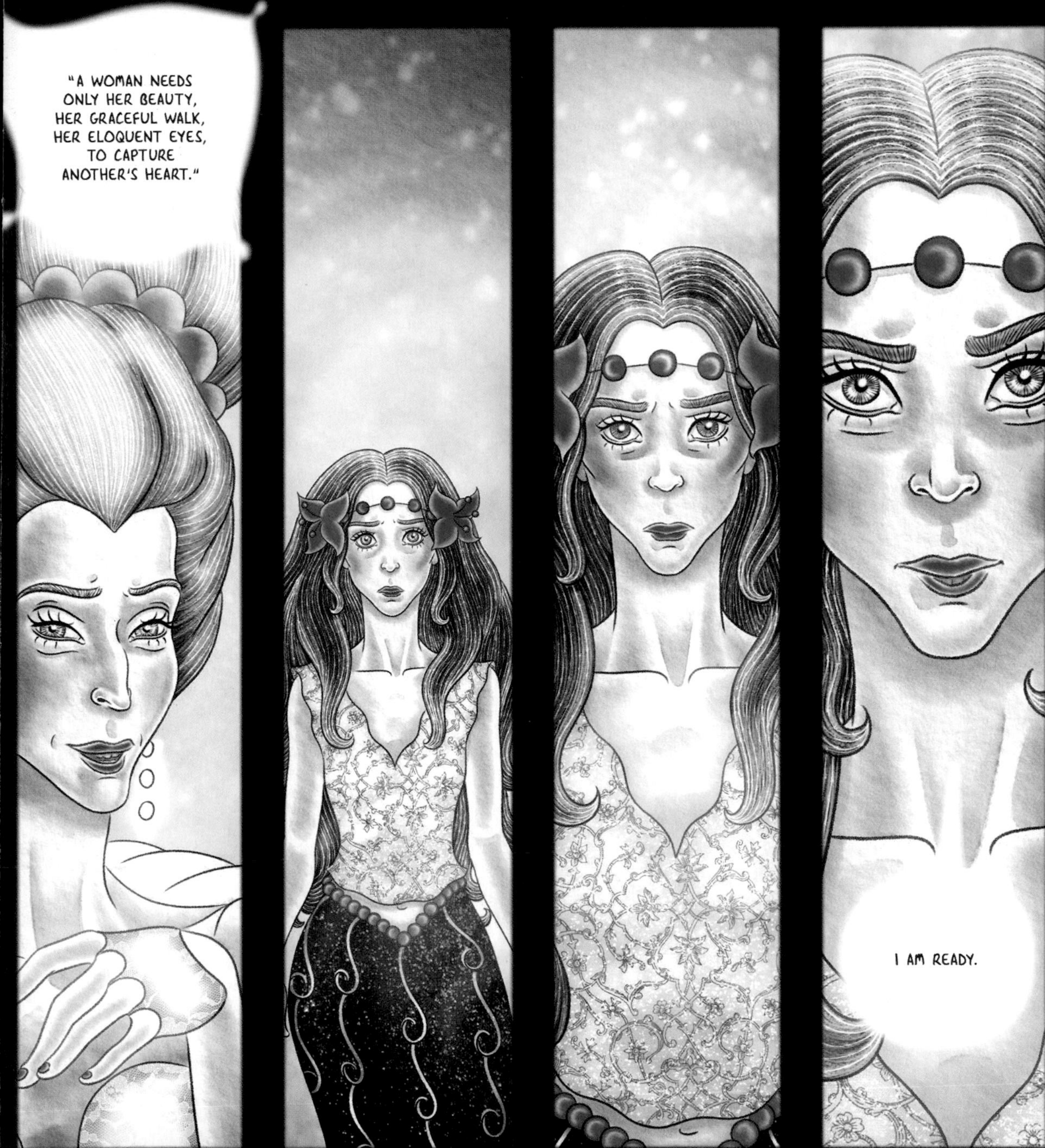
"A WOMAN NEEDS ONLY HER BEAUTY, HER GRACEFUL WALK, HER ELOQUENT EYES, TO CAPTURE ANOTHER'S HEART."
I AM READY.

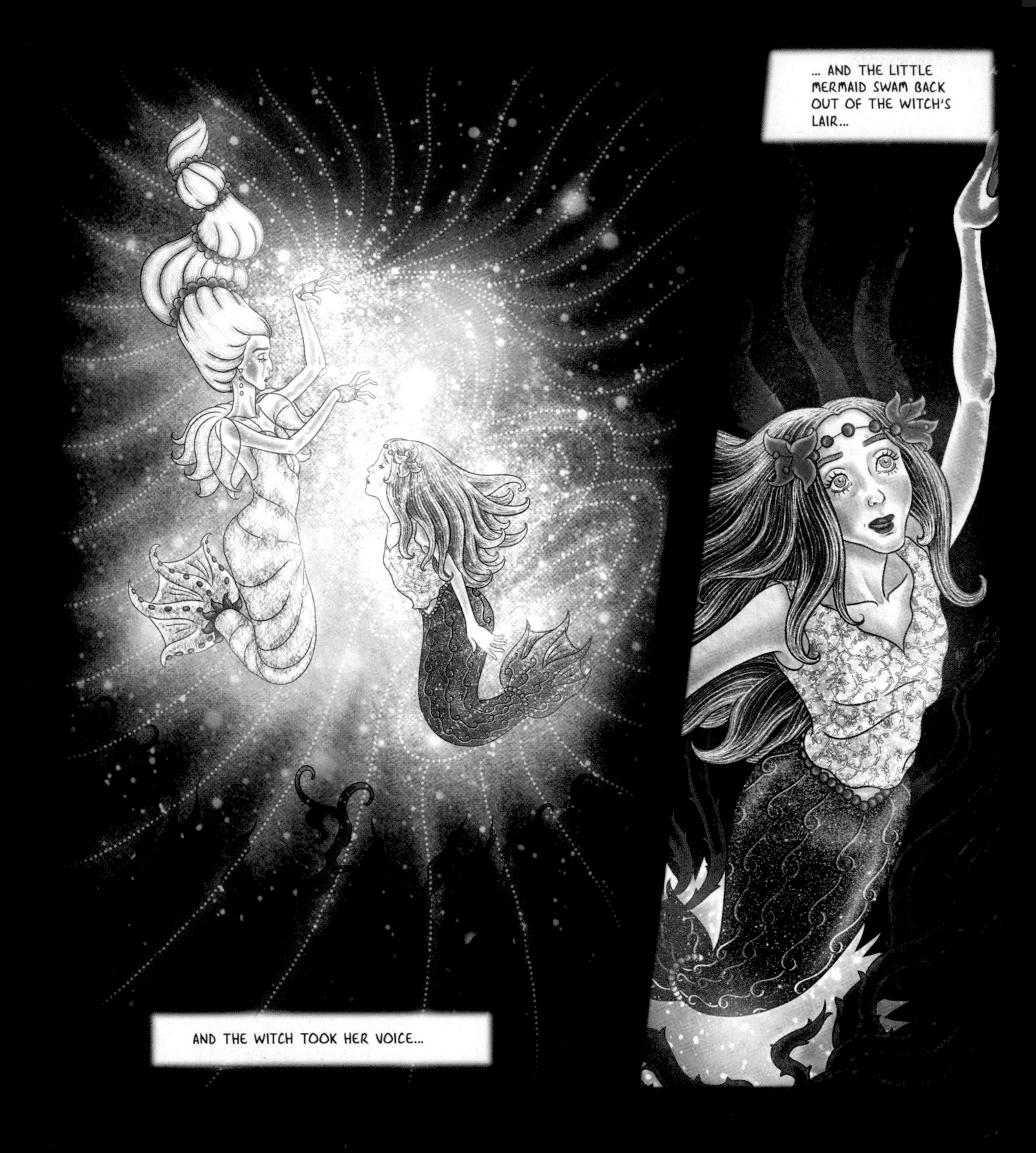
AND THE WITCH TOOK HER VOICE...
... AND THE LITTLE MERMAID SWAM BACK OUT OF THE WITCH'S LAIR...

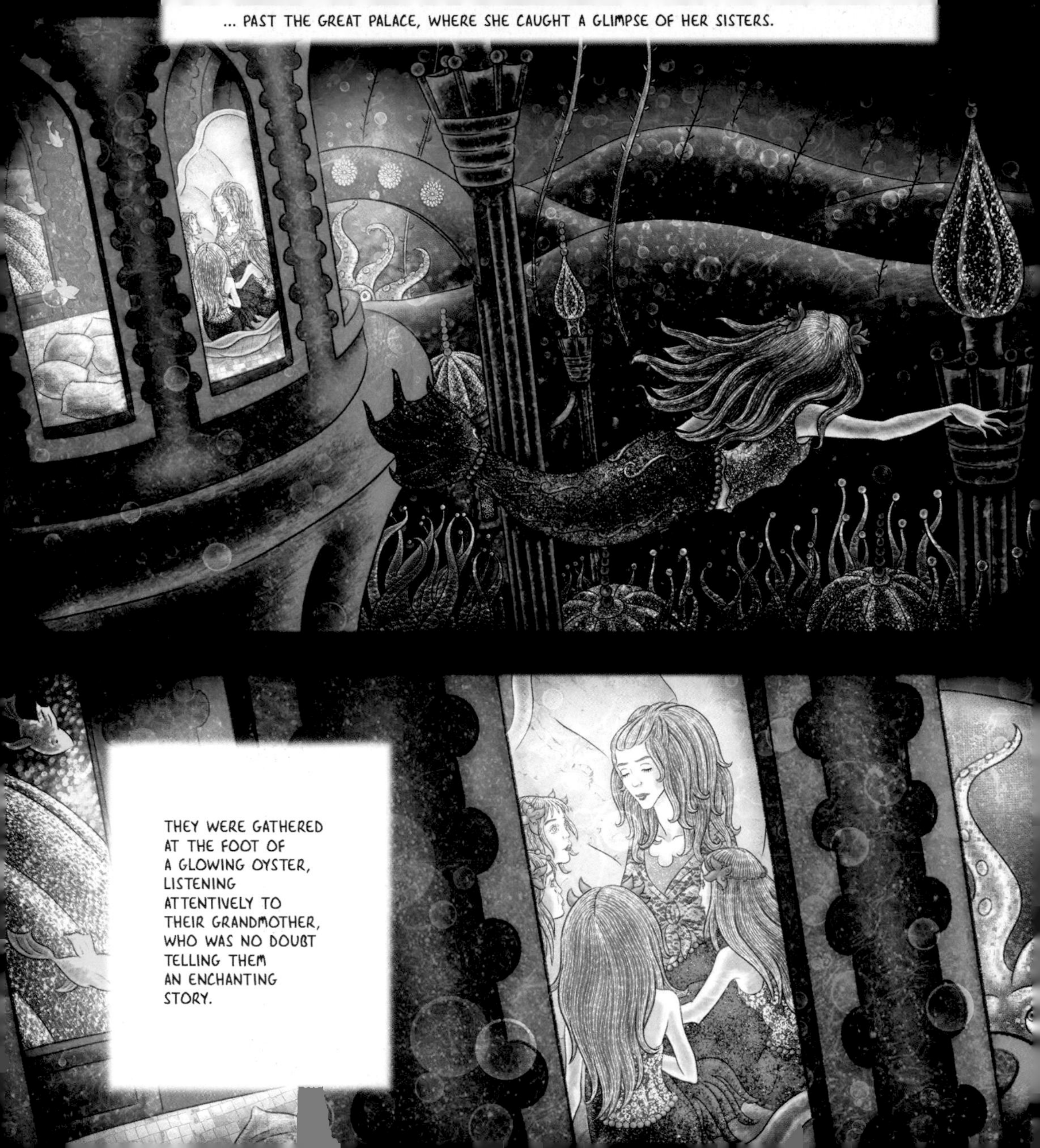
... PAST THE GREAT PALACE, WHERE SHE CAUGHT A GLIMPSE OF HER SISTERS.
THEY WERE GATHERED AT THE FOOT OF A GLOWING OYSTER, LISTENING ATTENTIVELY TO THEIR GRANDMOTHER, WHO WAS NO DOUBT TELLING THEM AN ENCHANTING STORY.

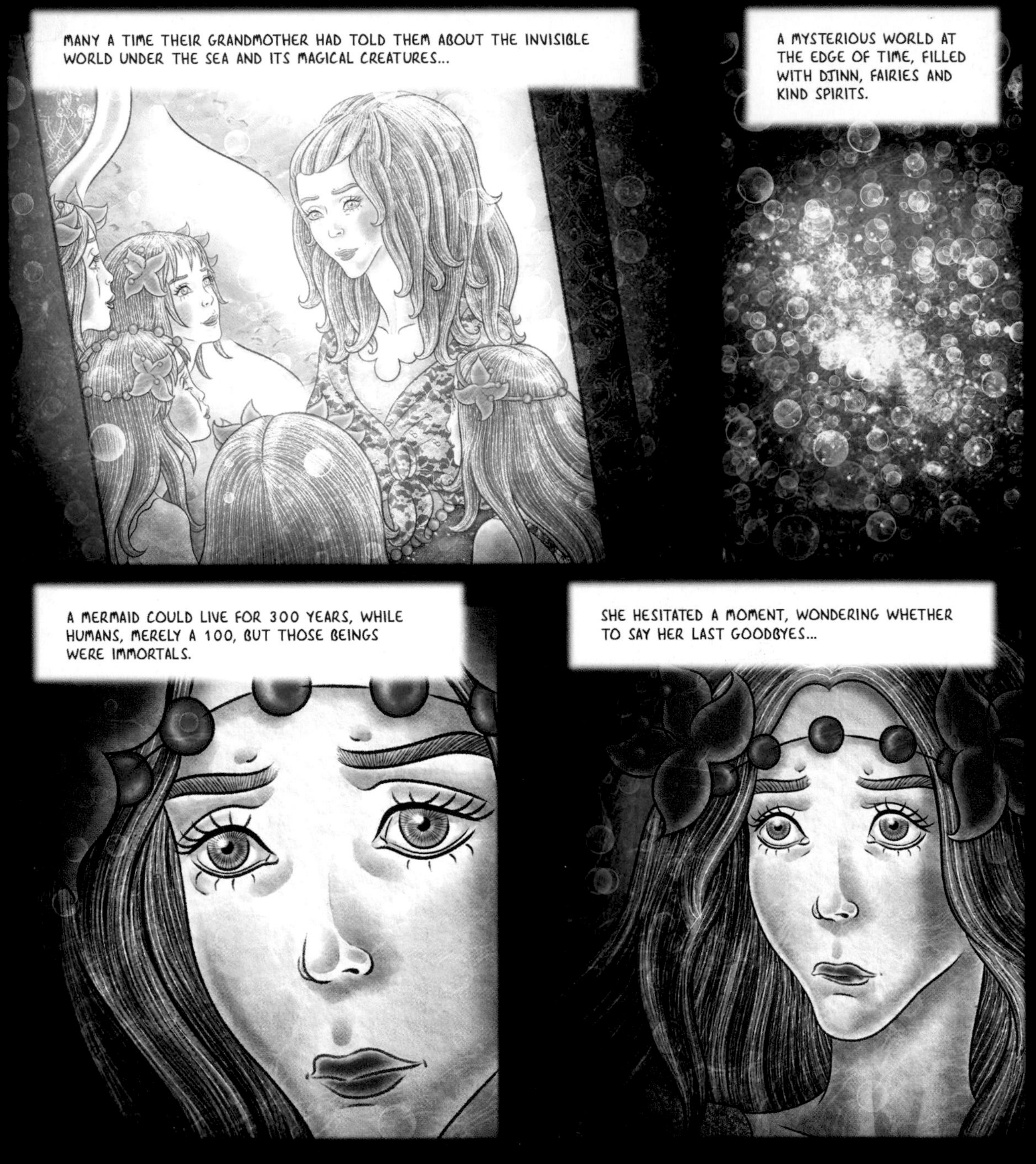
MANY A TIME THEIR GRANDMOTHER HAD TOLD THEM ABOUT THE INVISIBLE WORLD UNDER THE SEA AND ITS MAGICAL CREATURES...
A MYSTERIOUS WORLD AT THE EDGE OF TIME, FILLED WITH DJINN, FAIRIES AND KIND SPIRITS.
A MERMAID COULD LIVE FOR 300 YEARS, WHILE HUMANS, MERELY A 100, BUT THOSE BEINGS WERE IMMORTALS.
SHE HESITATED A MOMENT, WONDERING WHETHER TO SAY HER LAST GOODBYES...

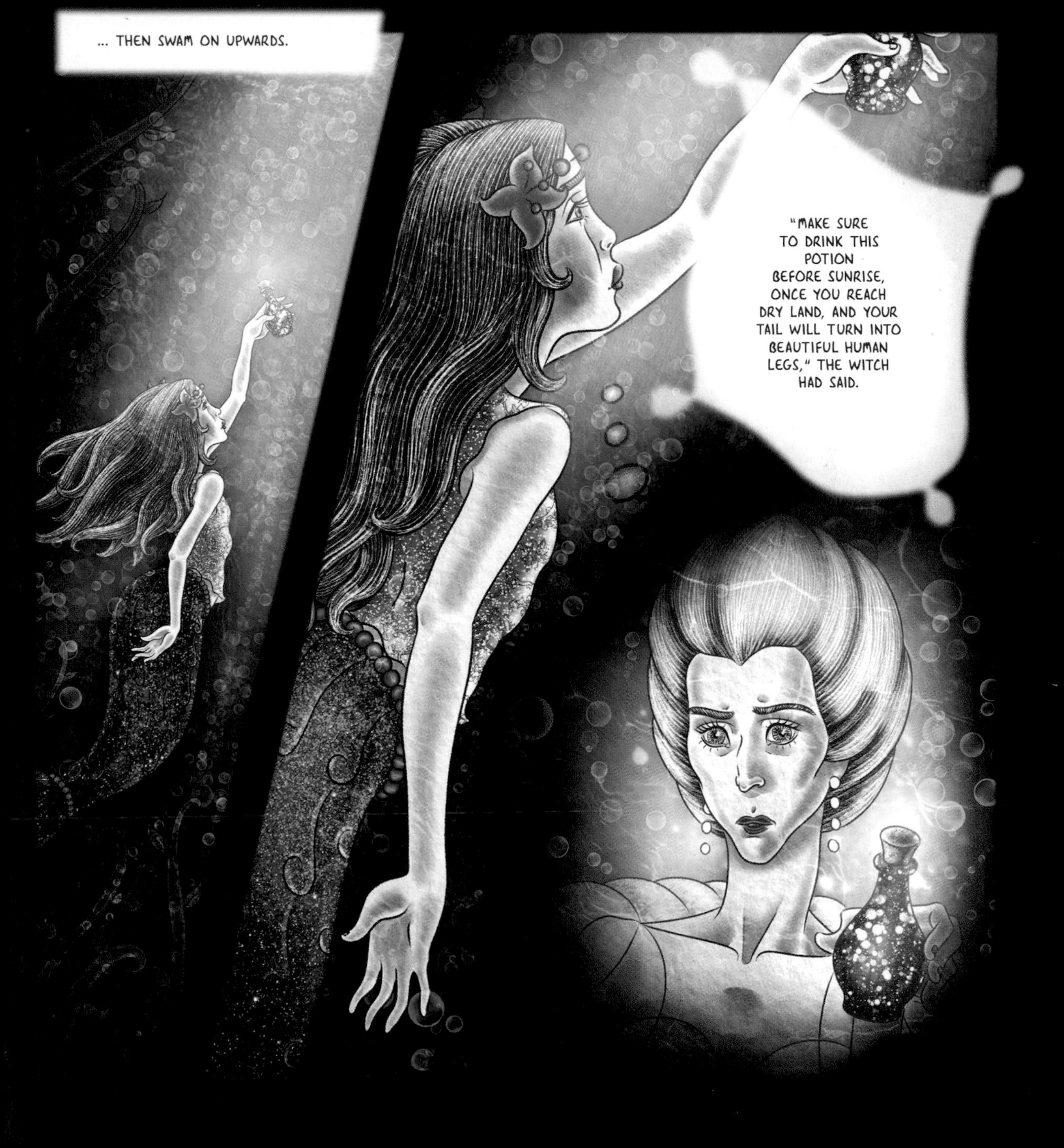
... THEN SWAM ON UPWARDS.
"MAKE SURE TO DRINK THIS POTION BEFORE SUNRISE, ONCE YOU REACH DRY LAND, AND YOUR TAIL WILL TURN INTO BEAUTIFUL HUMAN LEGS," THE WITCH HAD SAID.

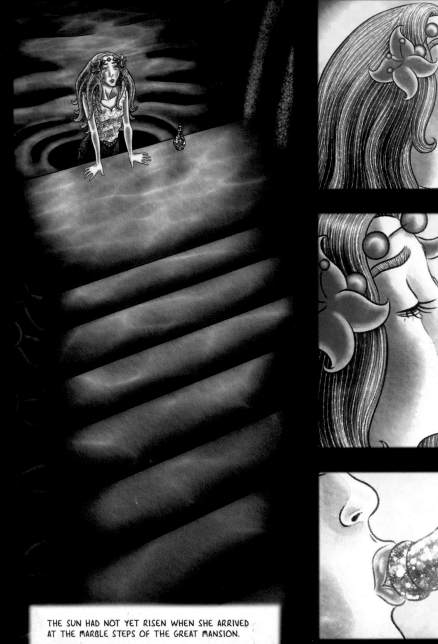

THE SUN HAD NOT YET RISEN WHEN SHE ARRIVED
AT THE MARBLE STEPS OF THE GREAT MANSION.

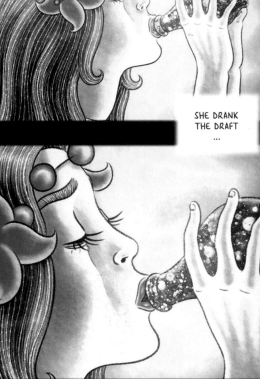

SHE DRANK
THE DRAFT
...

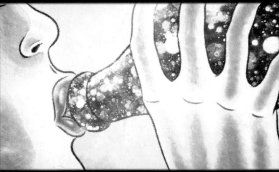

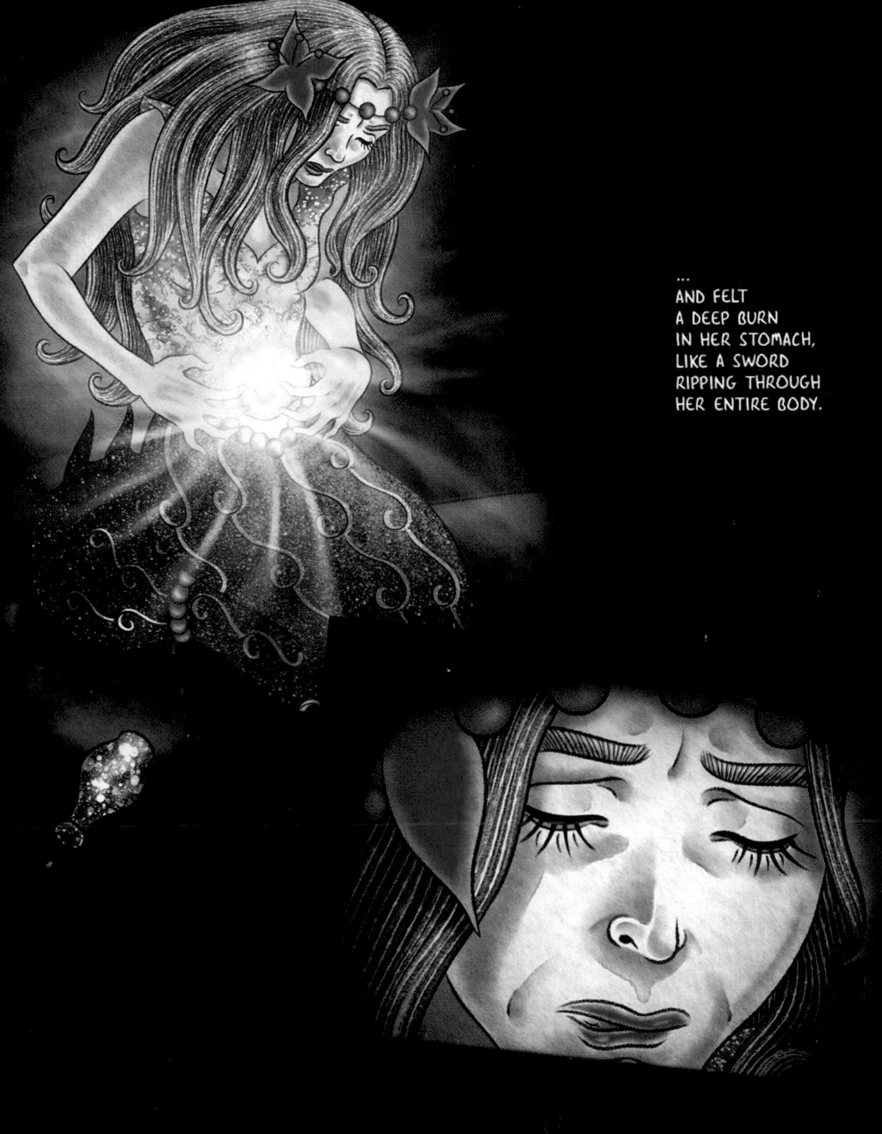
...
AND FELT
A DEEP BURN
IN HER STOMACH,
LIKE A SWORD
RIPPING THROUGH
HER ENTIRE BODY.

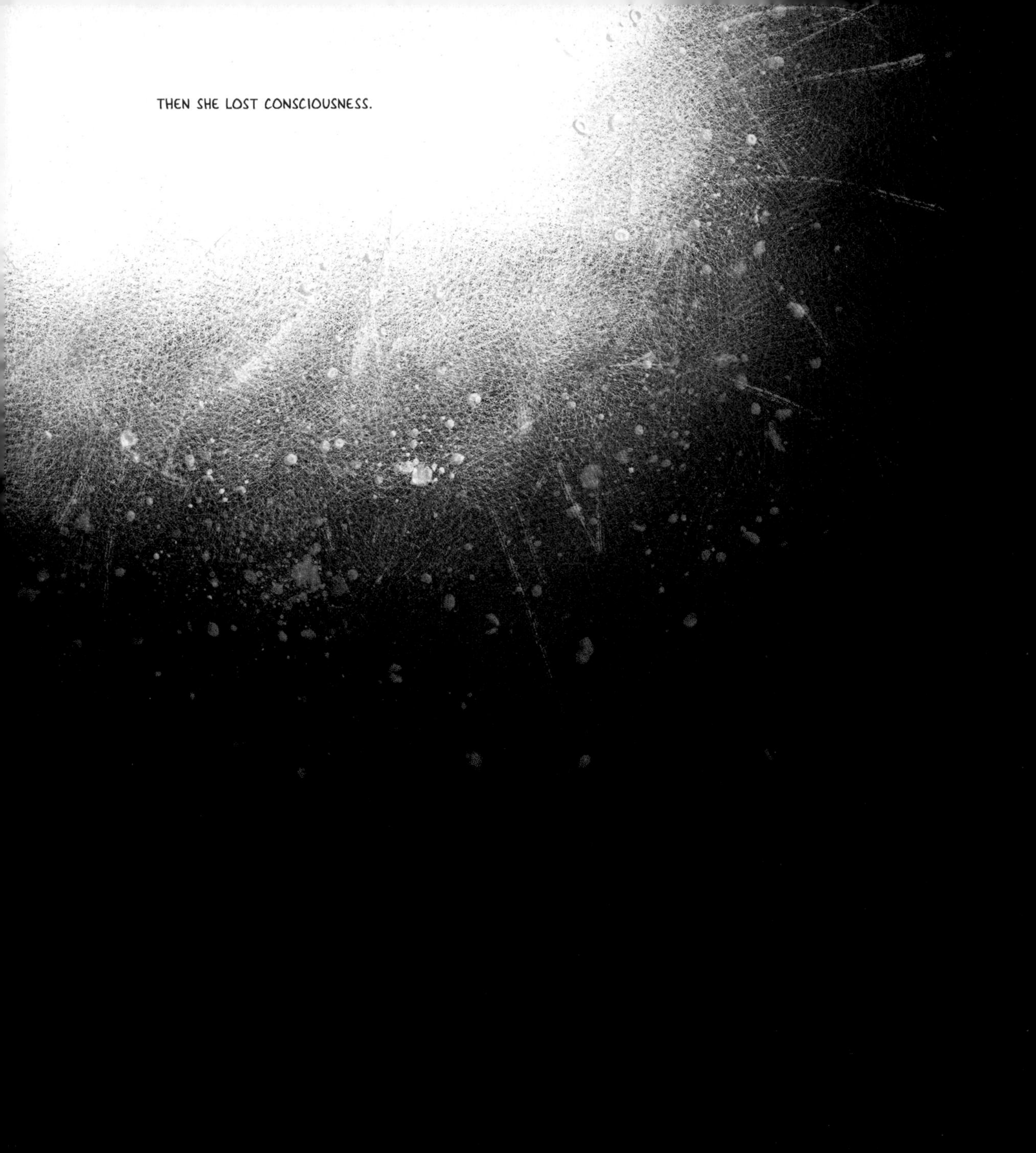
THEN SHE LOST CONSCIOUSNESS.

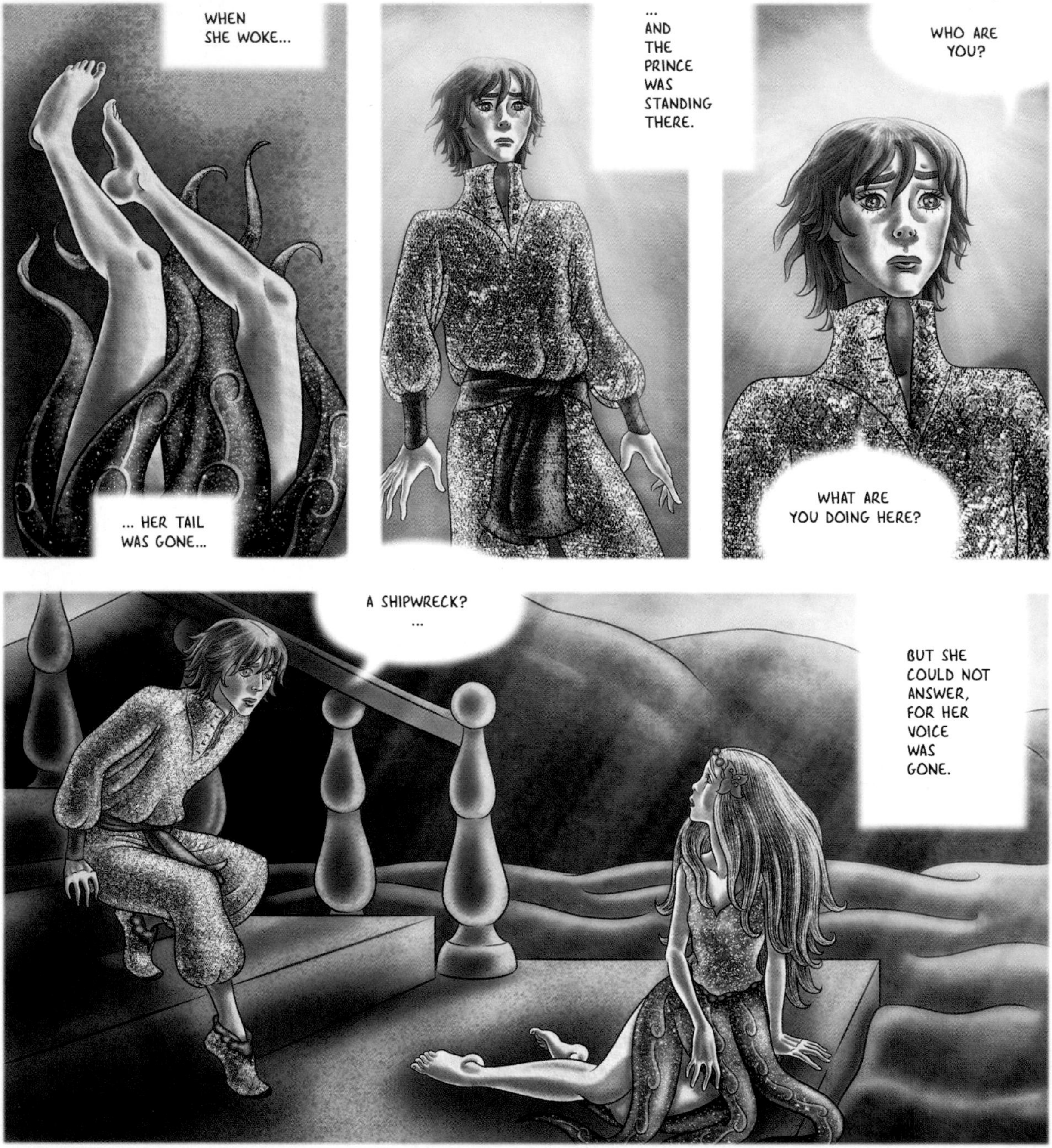
WHEN SHE WOKE...
... HER TAIL WAS GONE...
... AND THE PRINCE WAS STANDING THERE.
WHO ARE YOU?
WHAT ARE YOU DOING HERE?
A SHIPWRECK? ...
BUT SHE COULD NOT ANSWER, FOR HER VOICE WAS GONE.

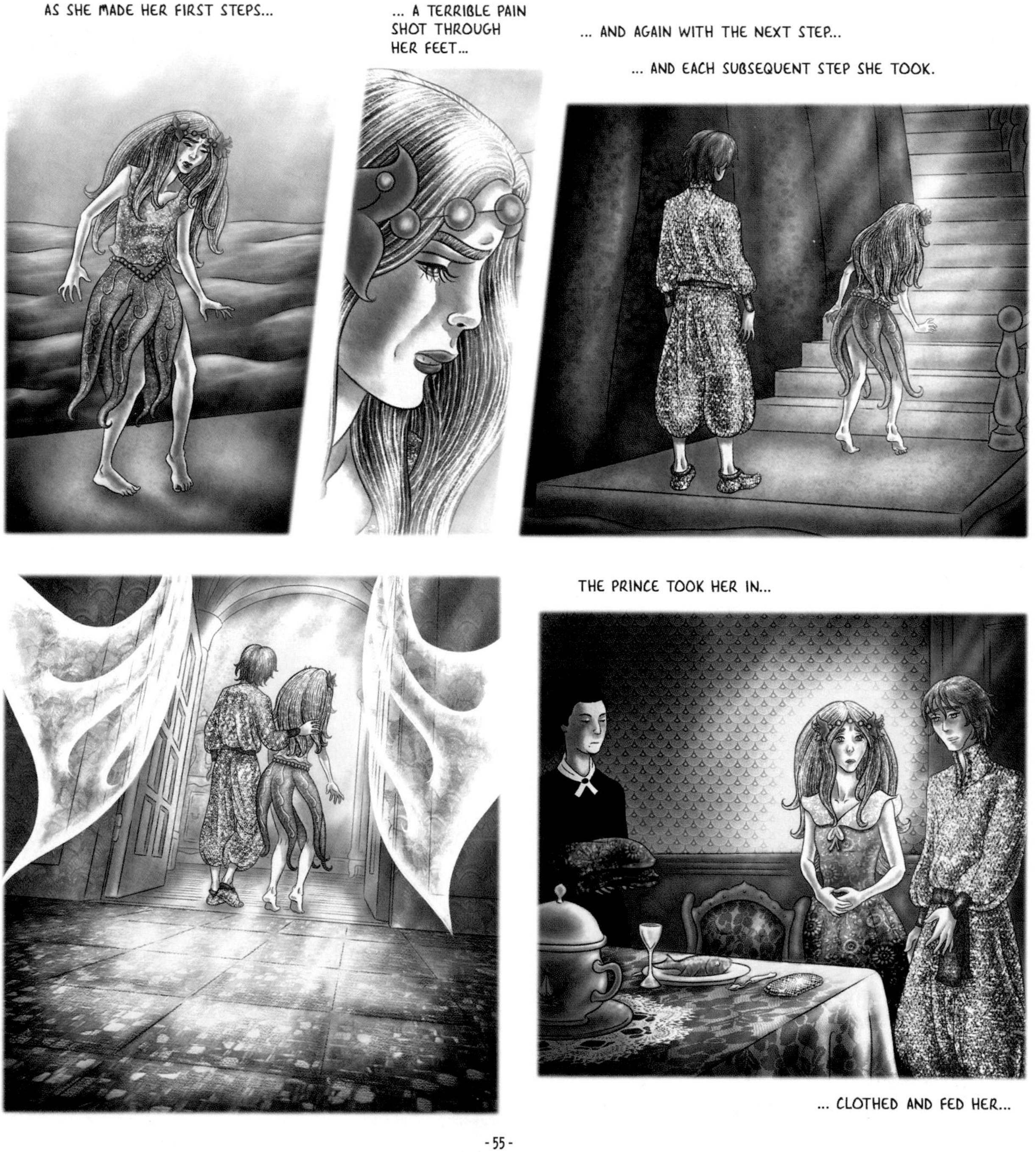
AS SHE MADE HER FIRST STEPS...
... A TERRIBLE PAIN SHOT THROUGH HER FEET...
... AND AGAIN WITH THE NEXT STEP...
... AND EACH SUBSEQUENT STEP SHE TOOK.
THE PRINCE TOOK HER IN...
... CLOTHED AND FED HER...

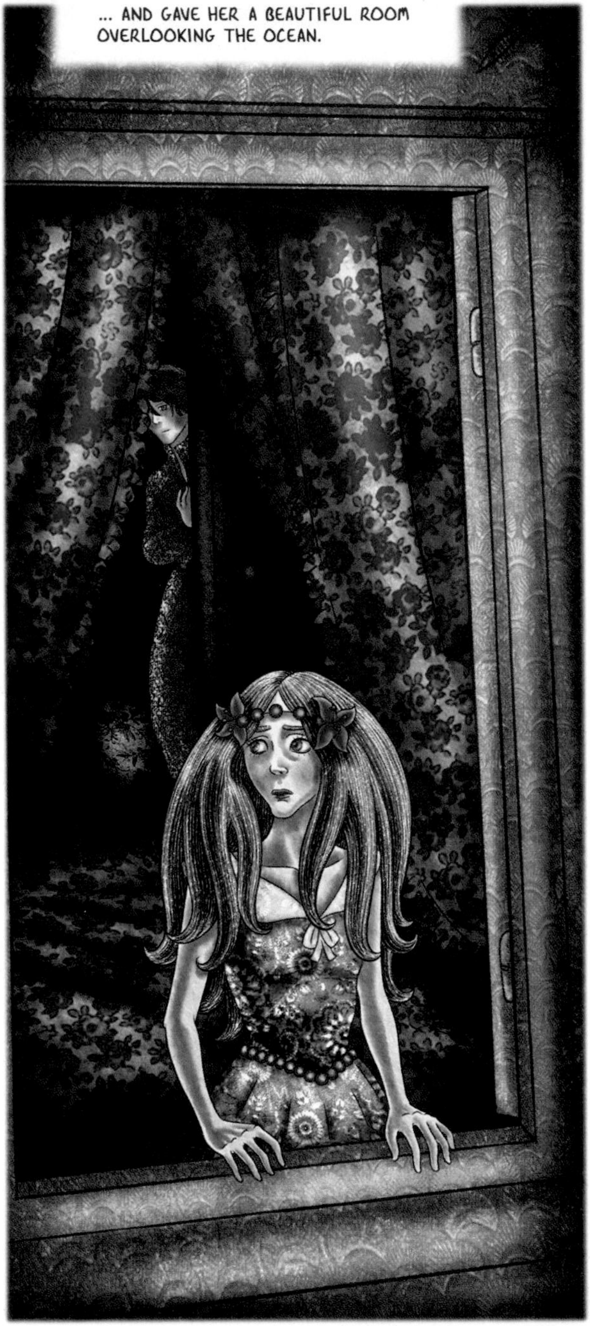
... AND GAVE HER A BEAUTIFUL ROOM OVERLOOKING THE OCEAN.

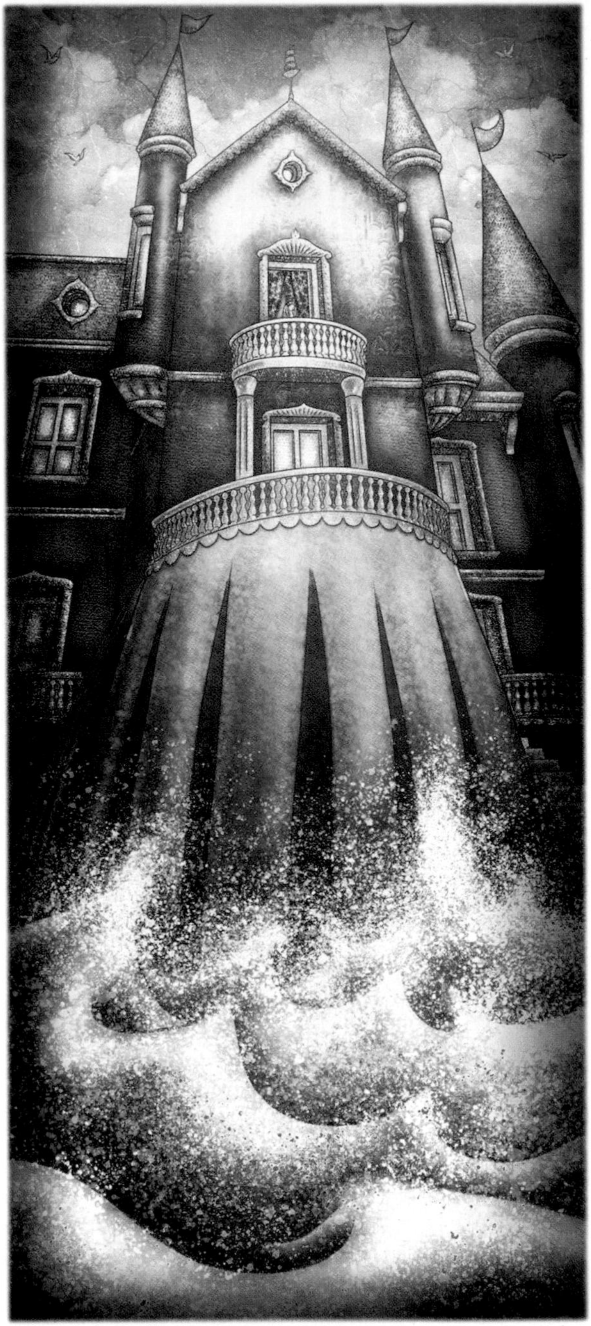

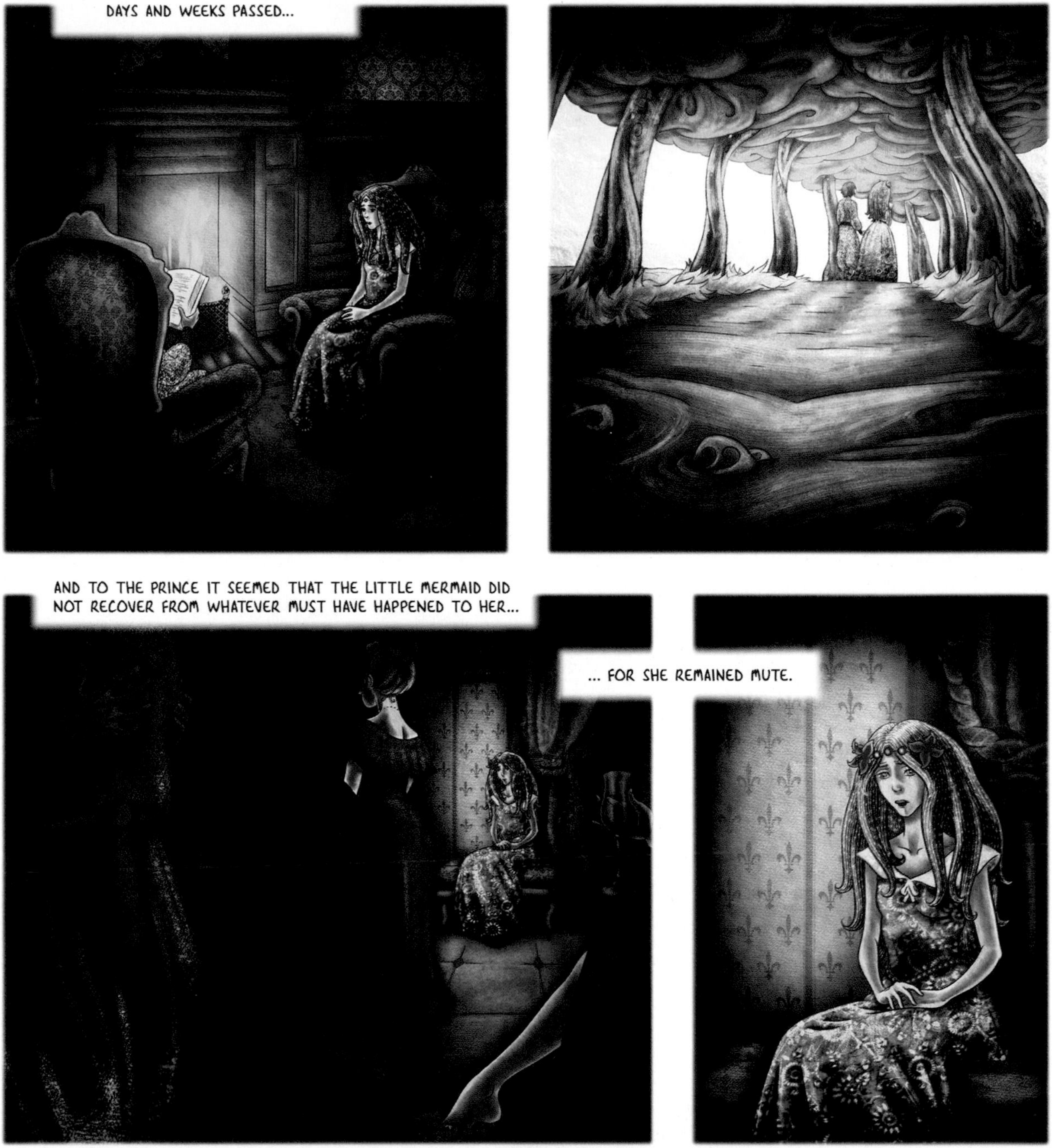
DAYS AND WEEKS PASSED...
AND TO THE PRINCE IT SEEMED THAT THE LITTLE MERMAID DID NOT RECOVER FROM WHATEVER MUST HAVE HAPPENED TO HER...
... FOR SHE REMAINED MUTE.

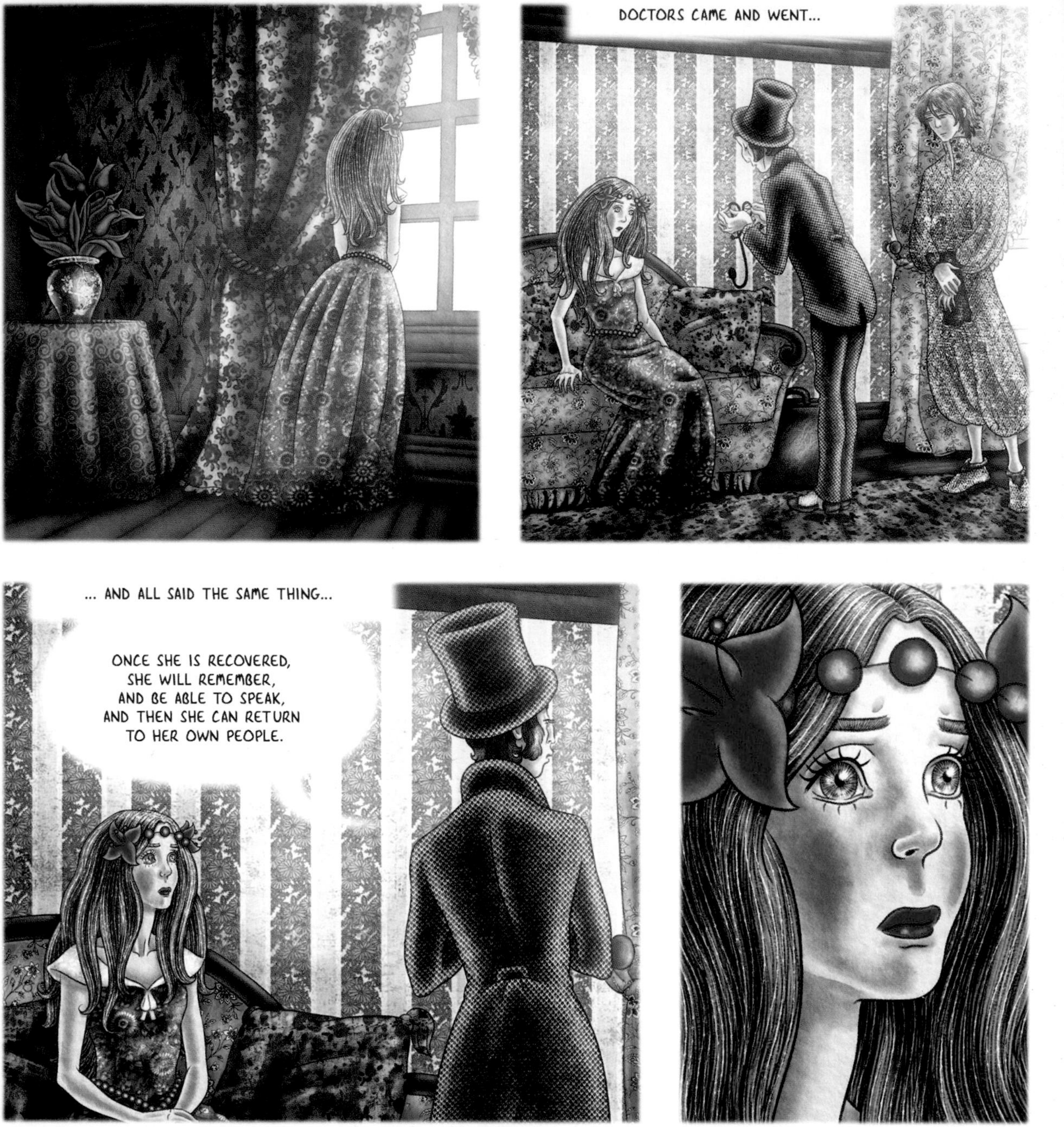
DOCTORS CAME AND WENT...
... AND ALL SAID THE SAME THING...
ONCE SHE IS RECOVERED, SHE WILL REMEMBER, AND BE ABLE TO SPEAK, AND THEN SHE CAN RETURN TO HER OWN PEOPLE.

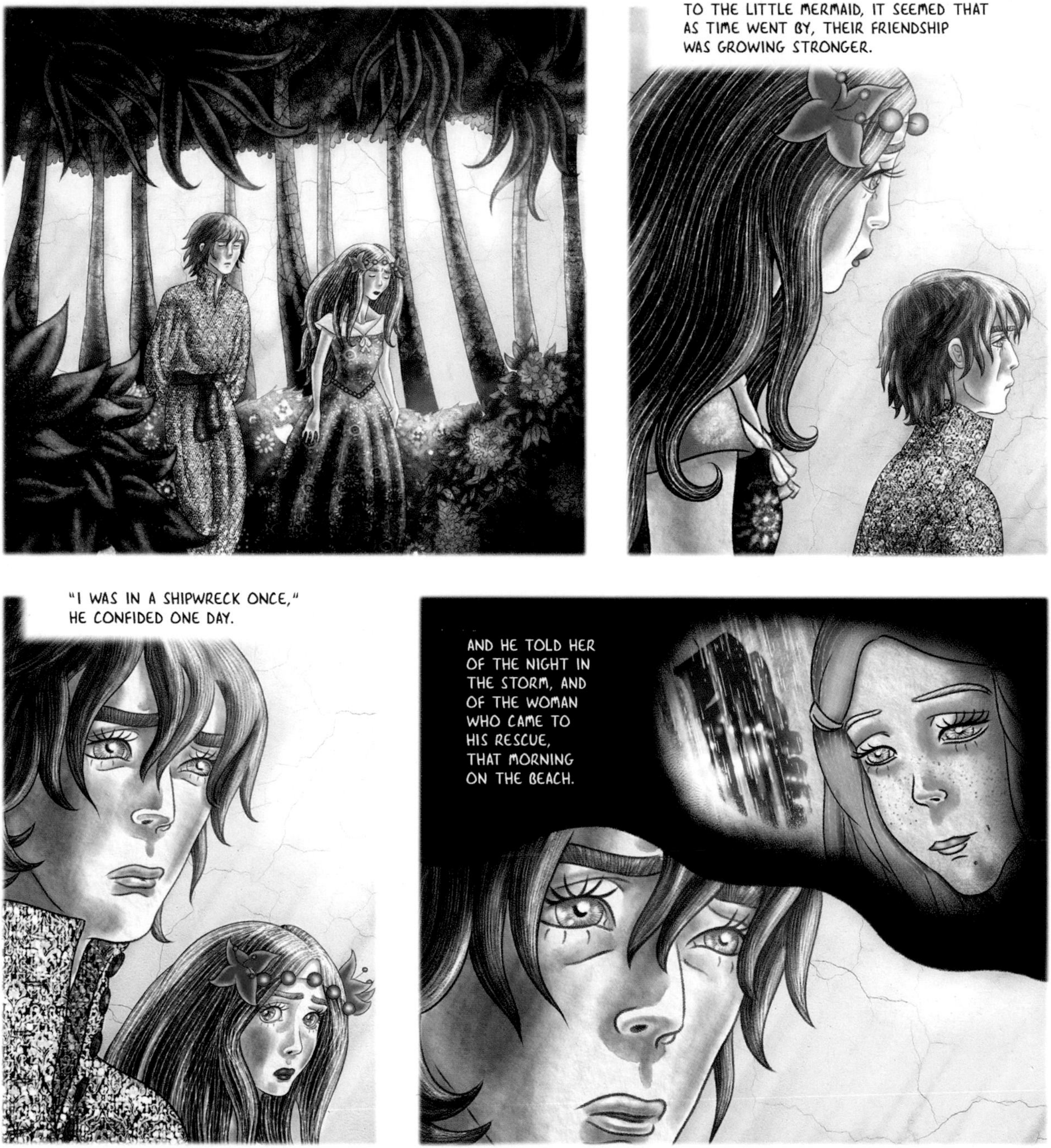
TO THE LITTLE MERMAID, IT SEEMED THAT AS TIME WENT BY, THEIR FRIENDSHIP WAS GROWING STRONGER.
"I WAS IN A SHIPWRECK ONCE," HE CONFIDED ONE DAY.
AND HE TOLD HER OF THE NIGHT IN THE STORM, AND OF THE WOMAN WHO CAME TO HIS RESCUE, THAT MORNING ON THE BEACH.

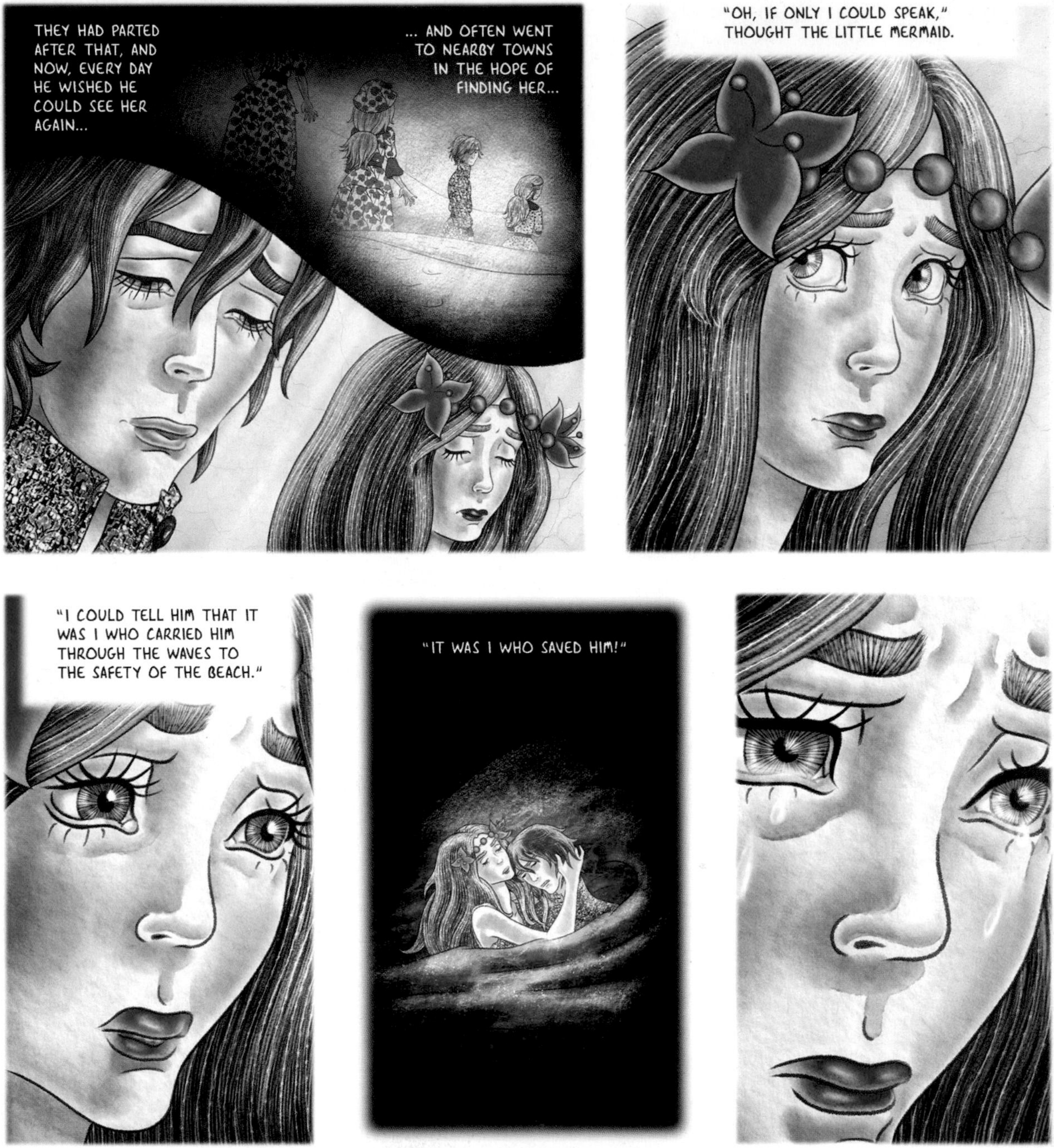
THEY HAD PARTED AFTER THAT, AND NOW, EVERY DAY HE WISHED HE COULD SEE HER AGAIN...
... AND OFTEN WENT TO NEARBY TOWNS IN THE HOPE OF FINDING HER...
"OH, IF ONLY I COULD SPEAK," THOUGHT THE LITTLE MERMAID.
"I COULD TELL HIM THAT IT WAS I WHO CARRIED HIM THROUGH THE WAVES TO THE SAFETY OF THE BEACH."
"IT WAS I WHO SAVED HIM!"

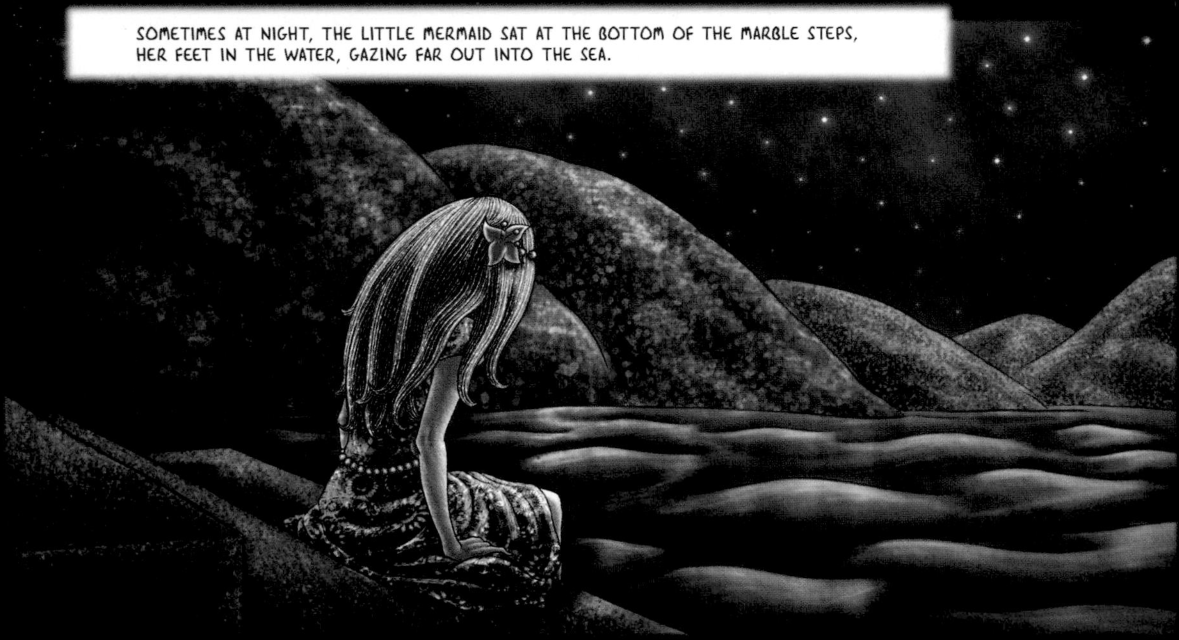
SOMETIMES AT NIGHT, THE LITTLE MERMAID SAT AT THE BOTTOM OF THE MARBLE STEPS, HER FEET IN THE WATER, GAZING FAR OUT INTO THE SEA.

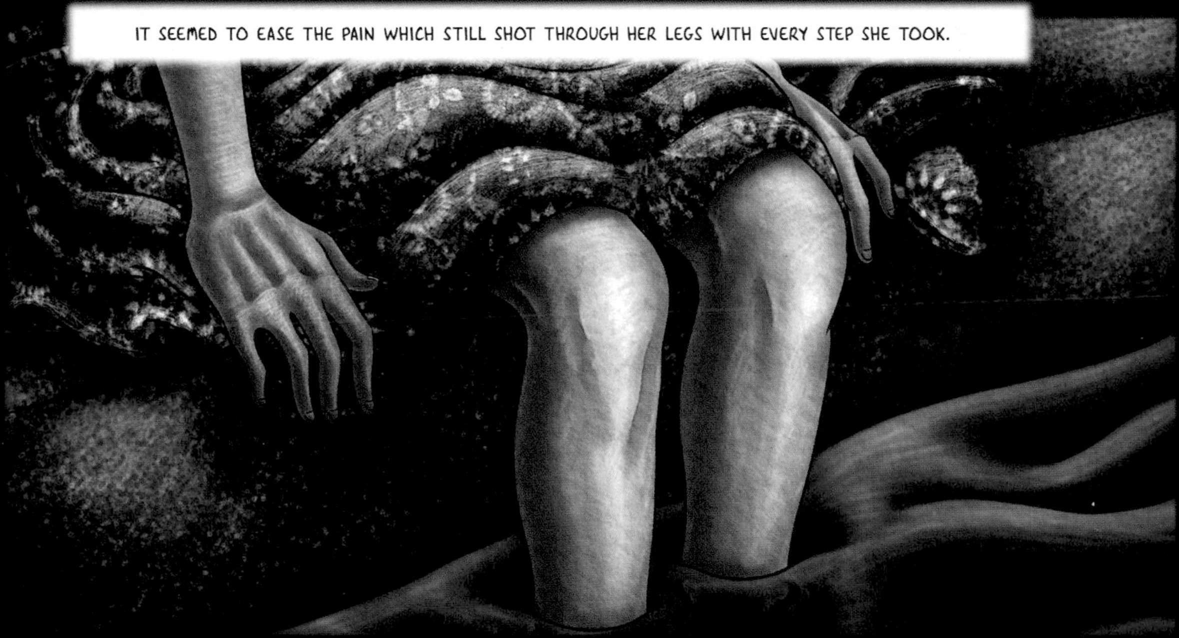
IT SEEMED TO EASE THE PAIN WHICH STILL SHOT THROUGH HER LEGS WITH EVERY STEP SHE TOOK.

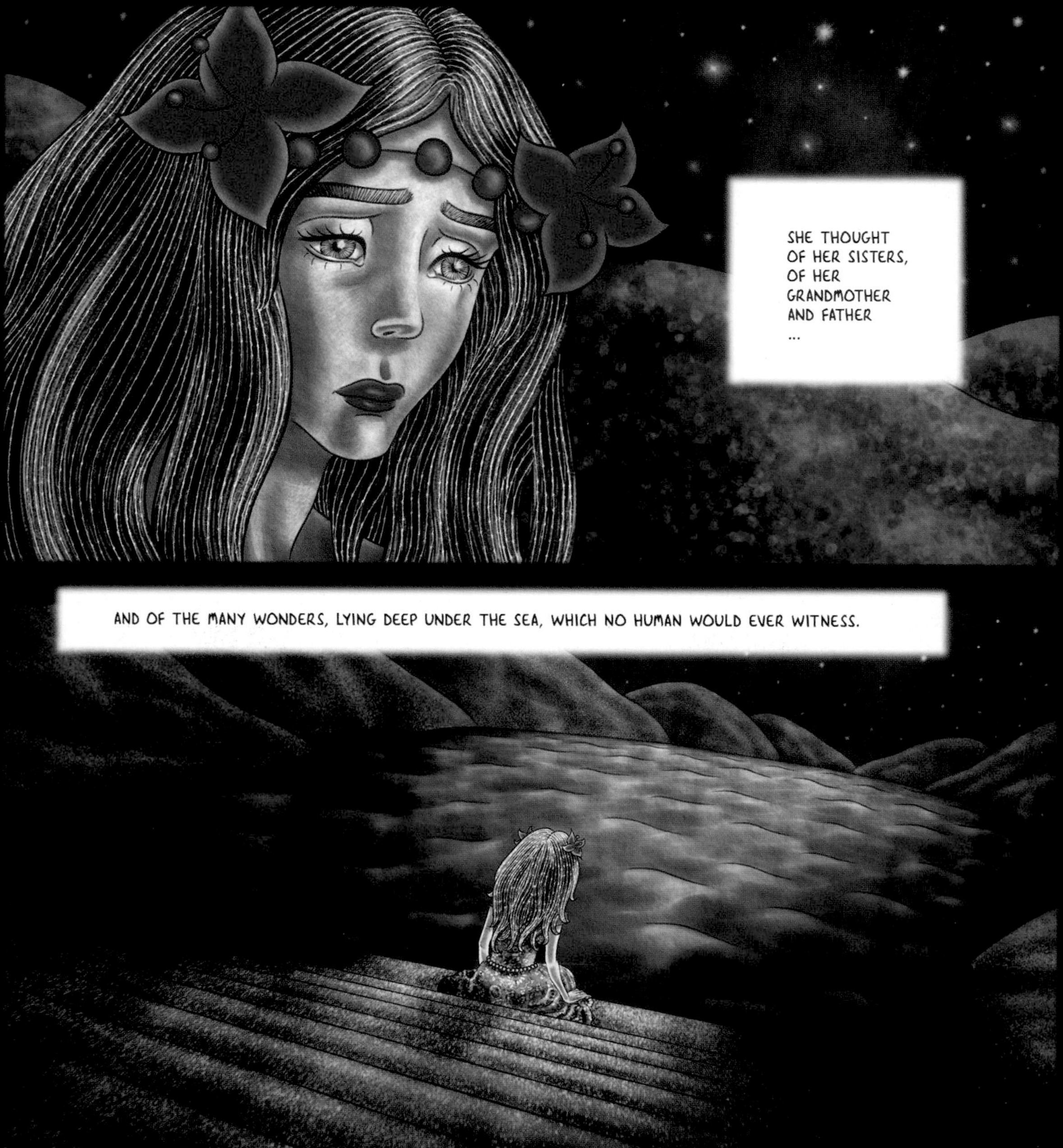

SHE THOUGHT OF HER SISTERS, OF HER GRANDMOTHER AND FATHER ...
AND OF THE MANY WONDERS, LYING DEEP UNDER THE SEA, WHICH NO HUMAN WOULD EVER WITNESS.

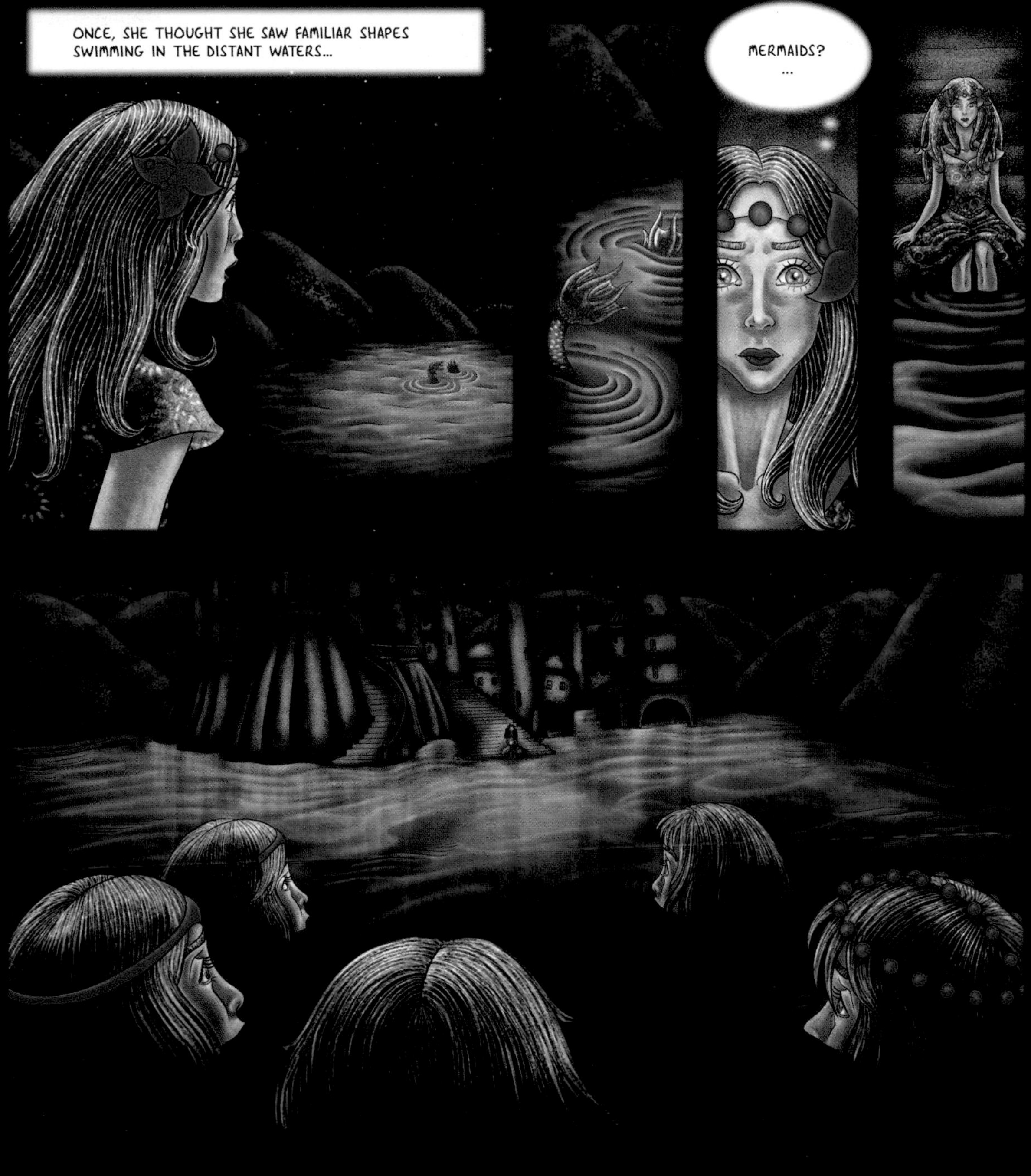
ONCE, SHE THOUGHT SHE SAW FAMILIAR SHAPES SWIMMING IN THE DISTANT WATERS...
MERMAIDS?
...

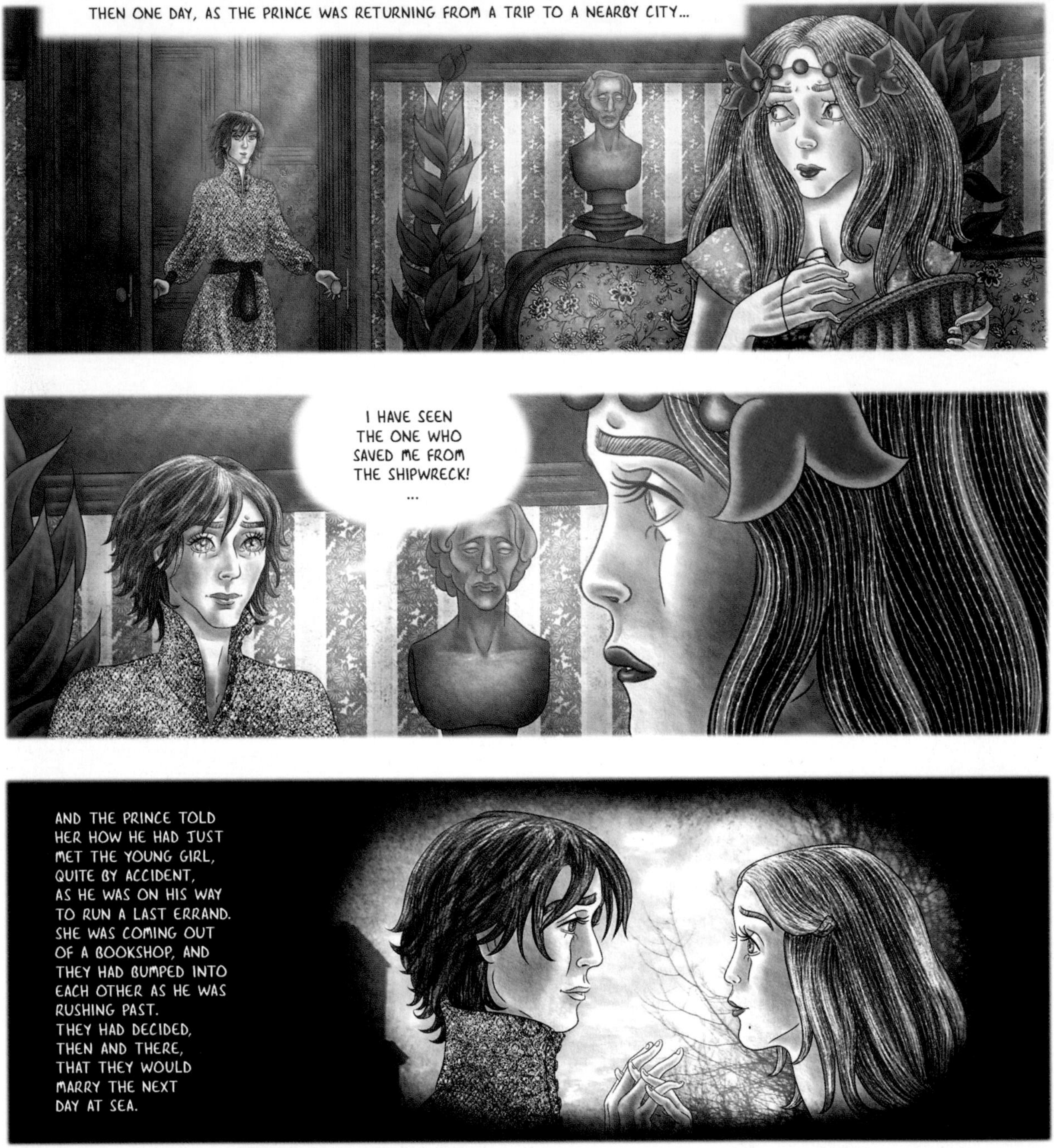
THEN ONE DAY, AS THE PRINCE WAS RETURNING FROM A TRIP TO A NEARBY CITY...
I HAVE SEEN THE ONE WHO SAVED ME FROM THE SHIPWRECK! ...
AND THE PRINCE TOLD HER HOW HE HAD JUST MET THE YOUNG GIRL, QUITE BY ACCIDENT, AS HE WAS ON HIS WAY TO RUN A LAST ERRAND. SHE WAS COMING OUT OF A BOOKSHOP, AND THEY HAD BUMPED INTO EACH OTHER AS HE WAS RUSHING PAST. THEY HAD DECIDED, THEN AND THERE, THAT THEY WOULD MARRY THE NEXT DAY AT SEA.

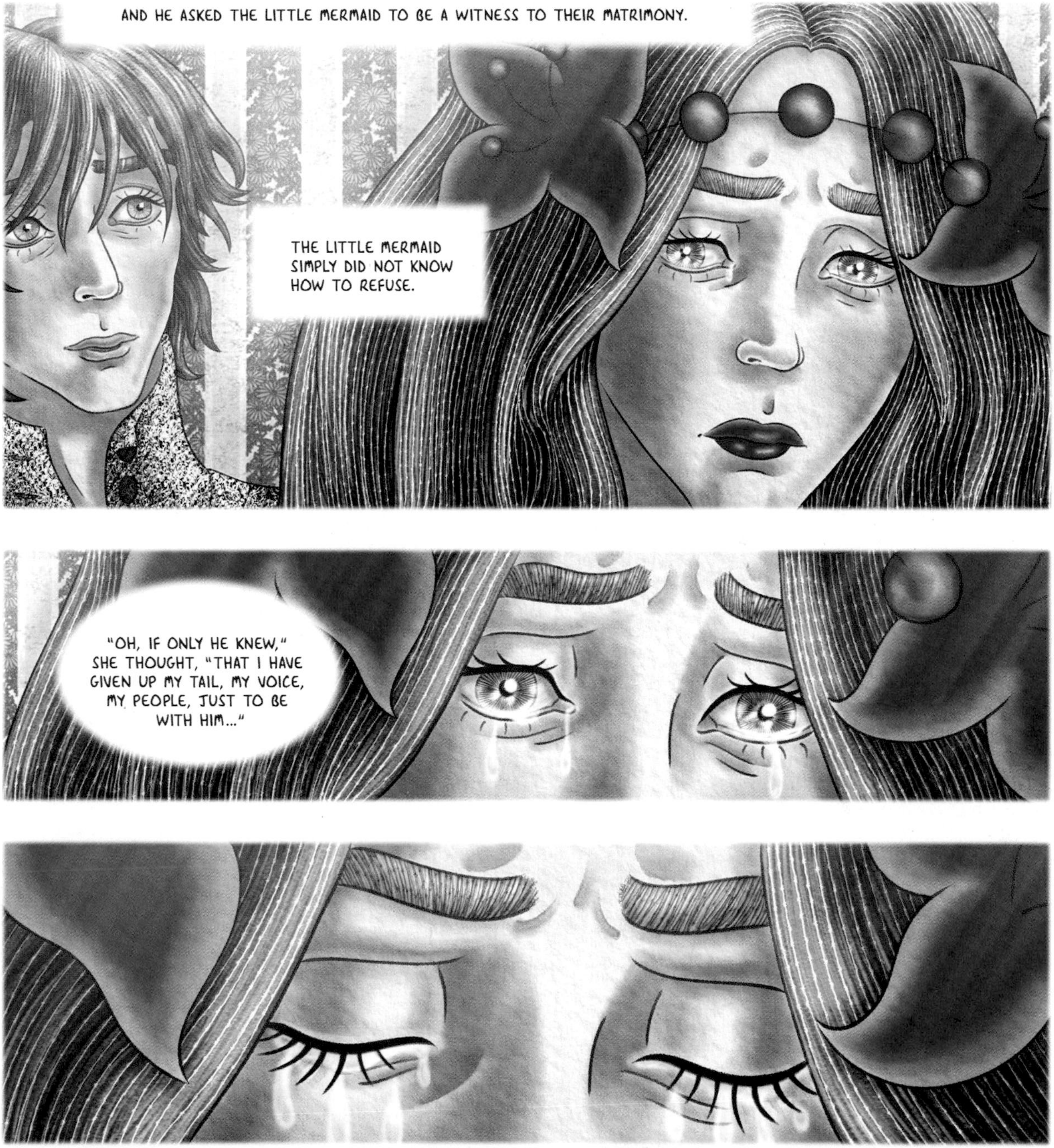
AND HE ASKED THE LITTLE MERMAID TO BE A WITNESS TO THEIR MATRIMONY.
THE LITTLE MERMAID SIMPLY DID NOT KNOW HOW TO REFUSE.
"OH, IF ONLY HE KNEW," SHE THOUGHT, "THAT I HAVE GIVEN UP MY TAIL, MY VOICE, MY PEOPLE, JUST TO BE WITH HIM..."

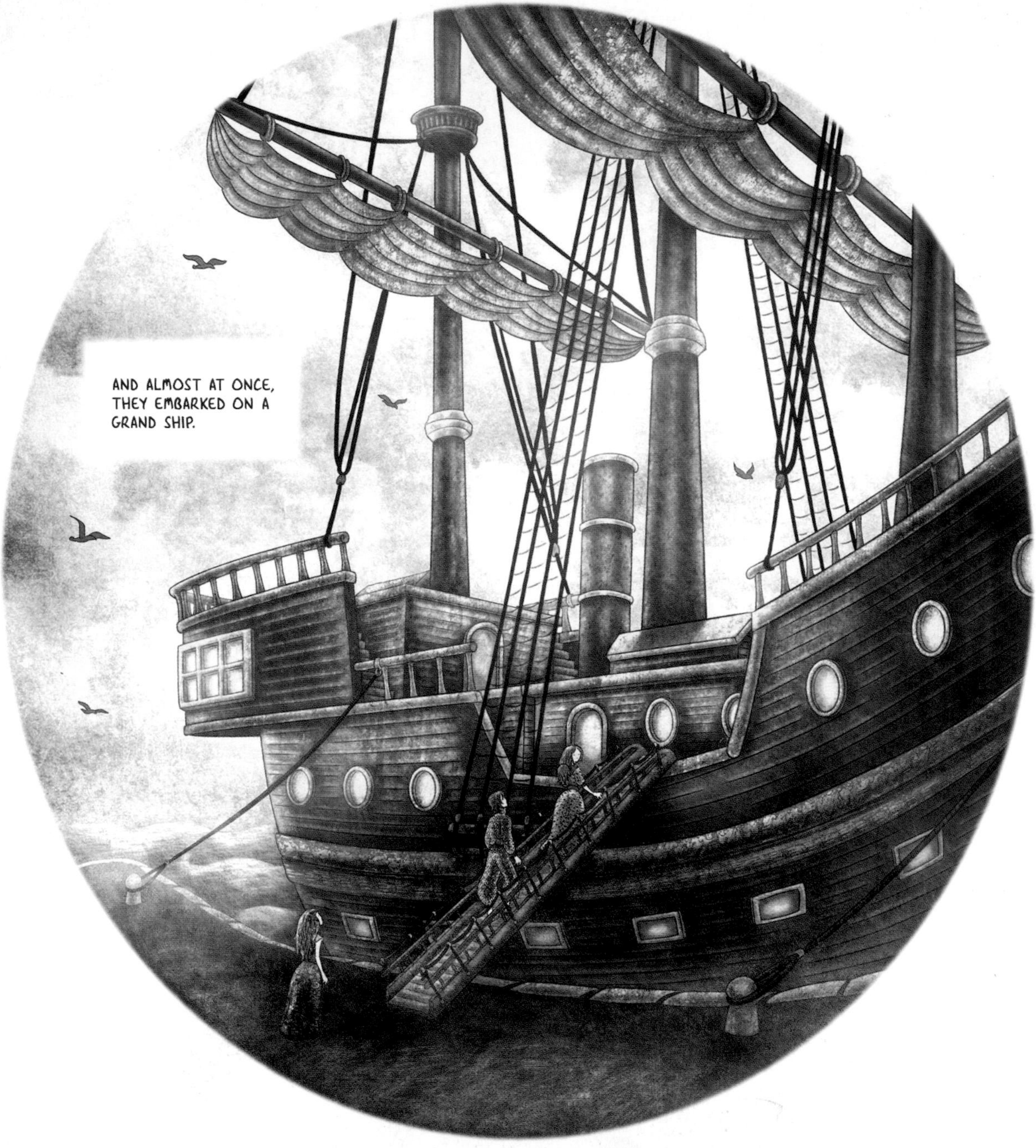
AND ALMOST AT ONCE, THEY EMBARKED ON A GRAND SHIP.

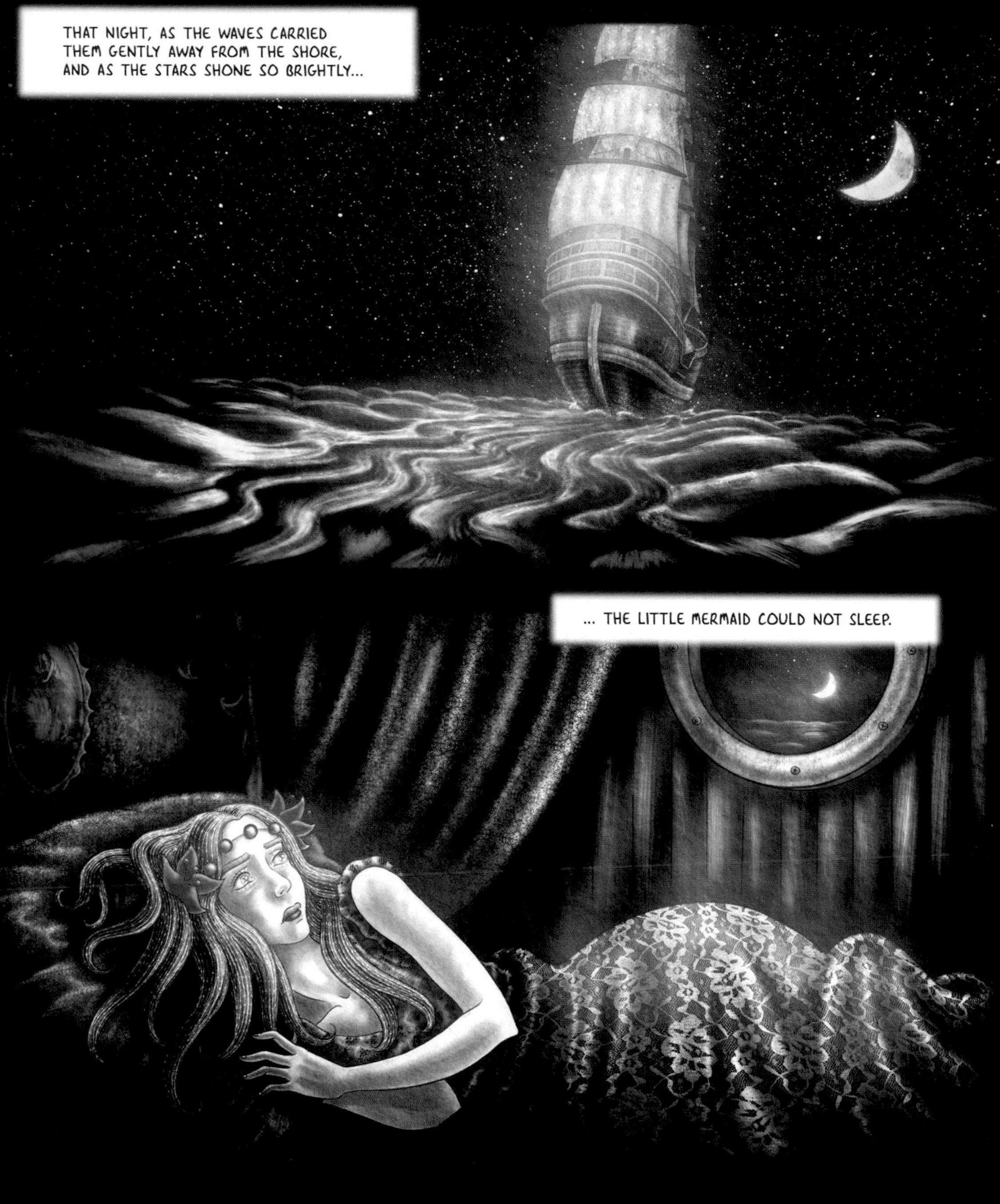
THAT NIGHT, AS THE WAVES CARRIED THEM GENTLY AWAY FROM THE SHORE, AND AS THE STARS SHONE SO BRIGHTLY...
... THE LITTLE MERMAID COULD NOT SLEEP.

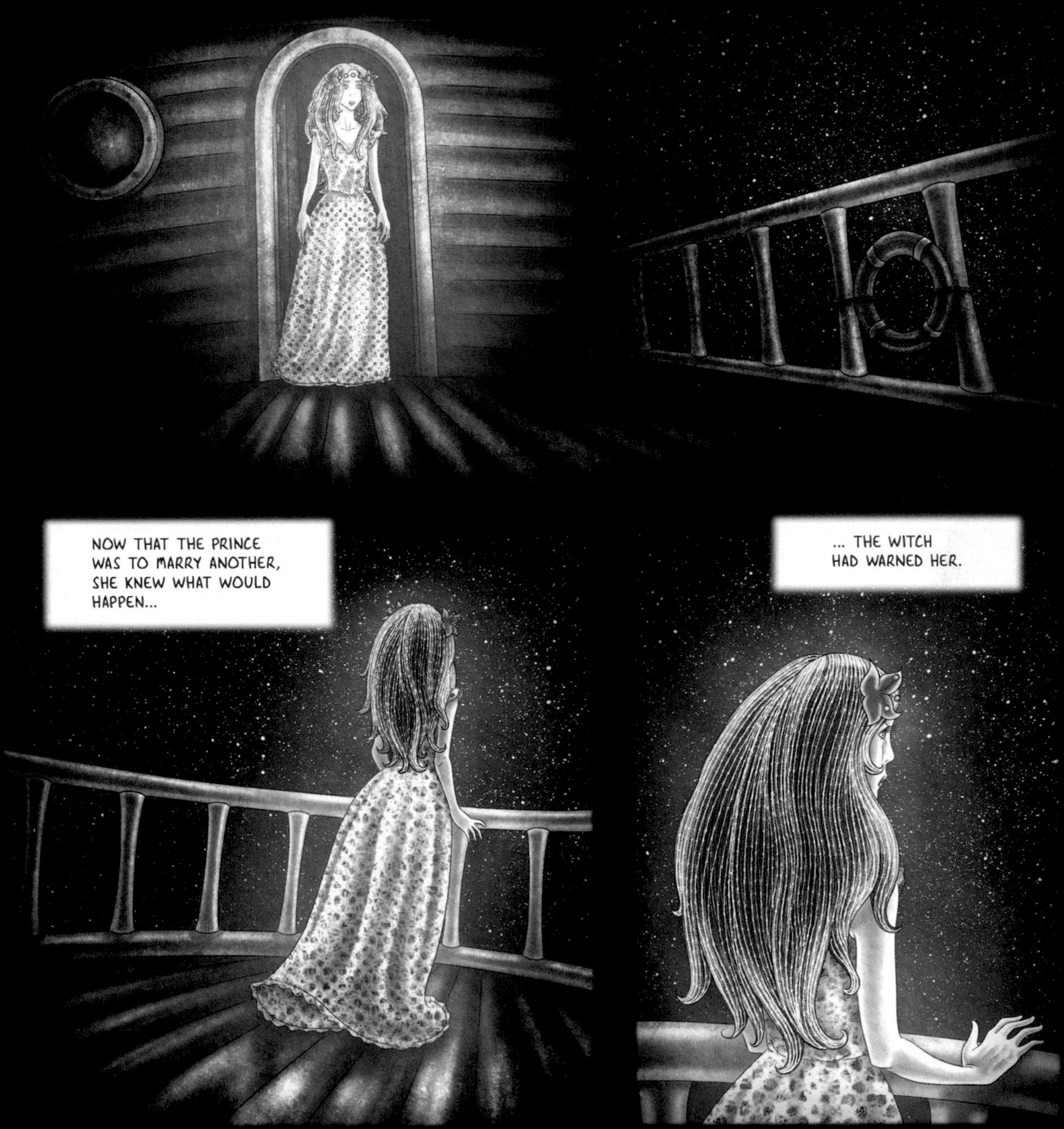
NOW THAT THE PRINCE WAS TO MARRY ANOTHER, SHE KNEW WHAT WOULD HAPPEN...
... THE WITCH HAD WARNED HER.

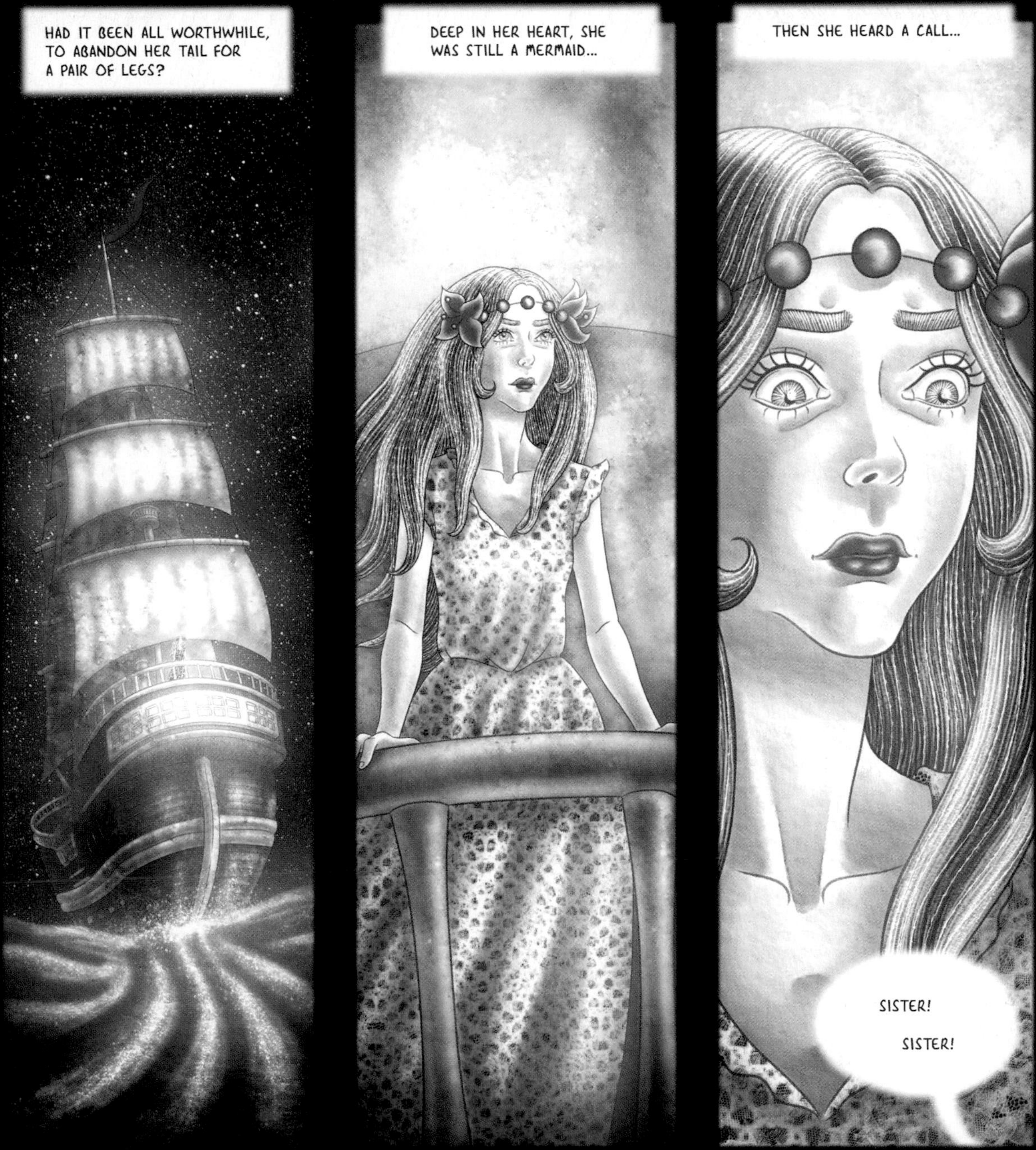
HAD IT BEEN ALL WORTHWHILE, TO ABANDON HER TAIL FOR A PAIR OF LEGS?
DEEP IN HER HEART, SHE WAS STILL A MERMAID...
THEN SHE HEARD A CALL...
SISTER! SISTER!

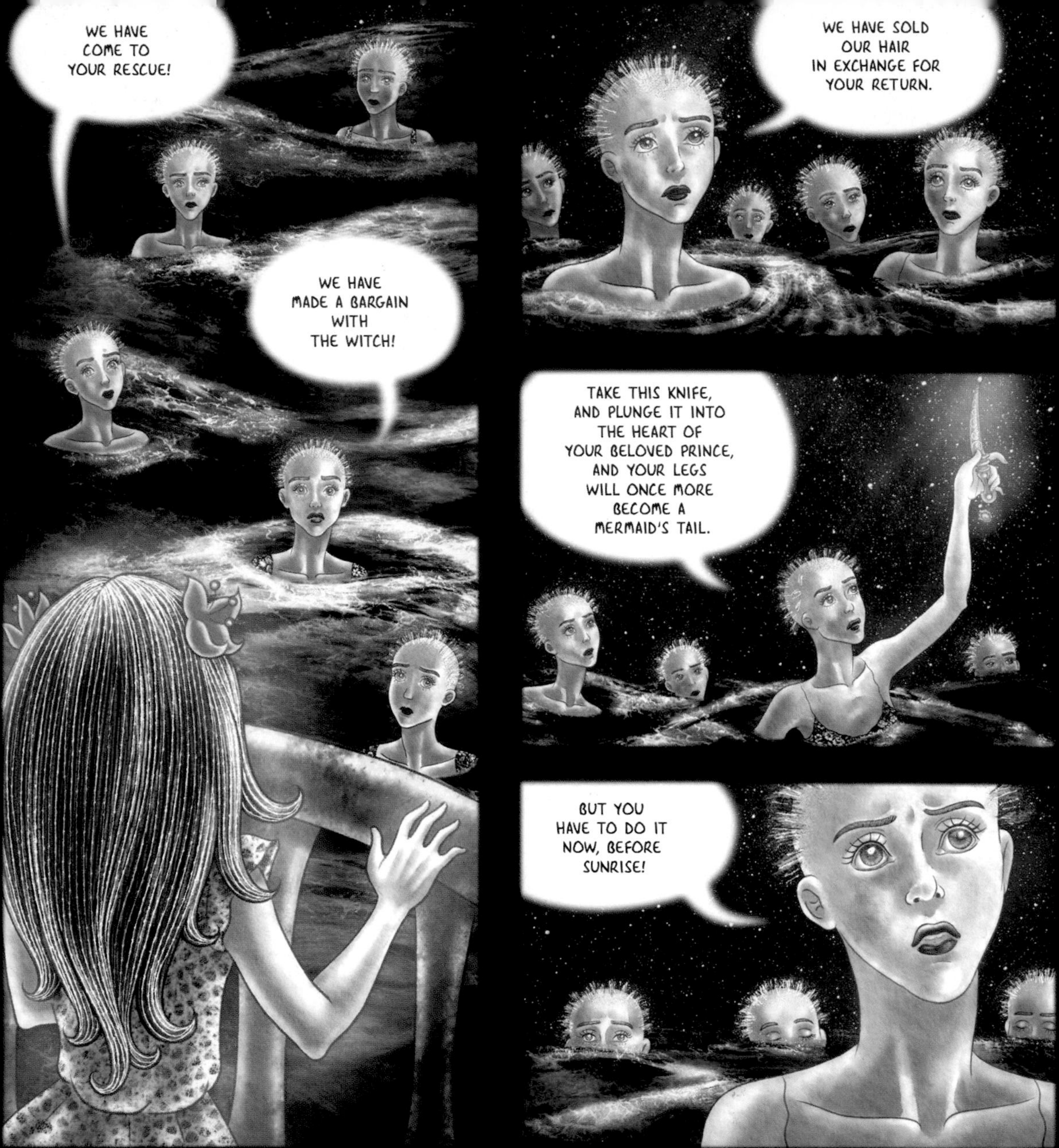
WE HAVE COME TO YOUR RESCUE!
WE HAVE MADE A BARGAIN WITH THE WITCH!
WE HAVE SOLD OUR HAIR IN EXCHANGE FOR YOUR RETURN.
TAKE THIS KNIFE, AND PLUNGE IT INTO THE HEART OF YOUR BELOVED PRINCE, AND YOUR LEGS WILL ONCE MORE BECOME A MERMAID'S TAIL.
BUT YOU HAVE TO DO IT NOW, BEFORE SUNRISE!

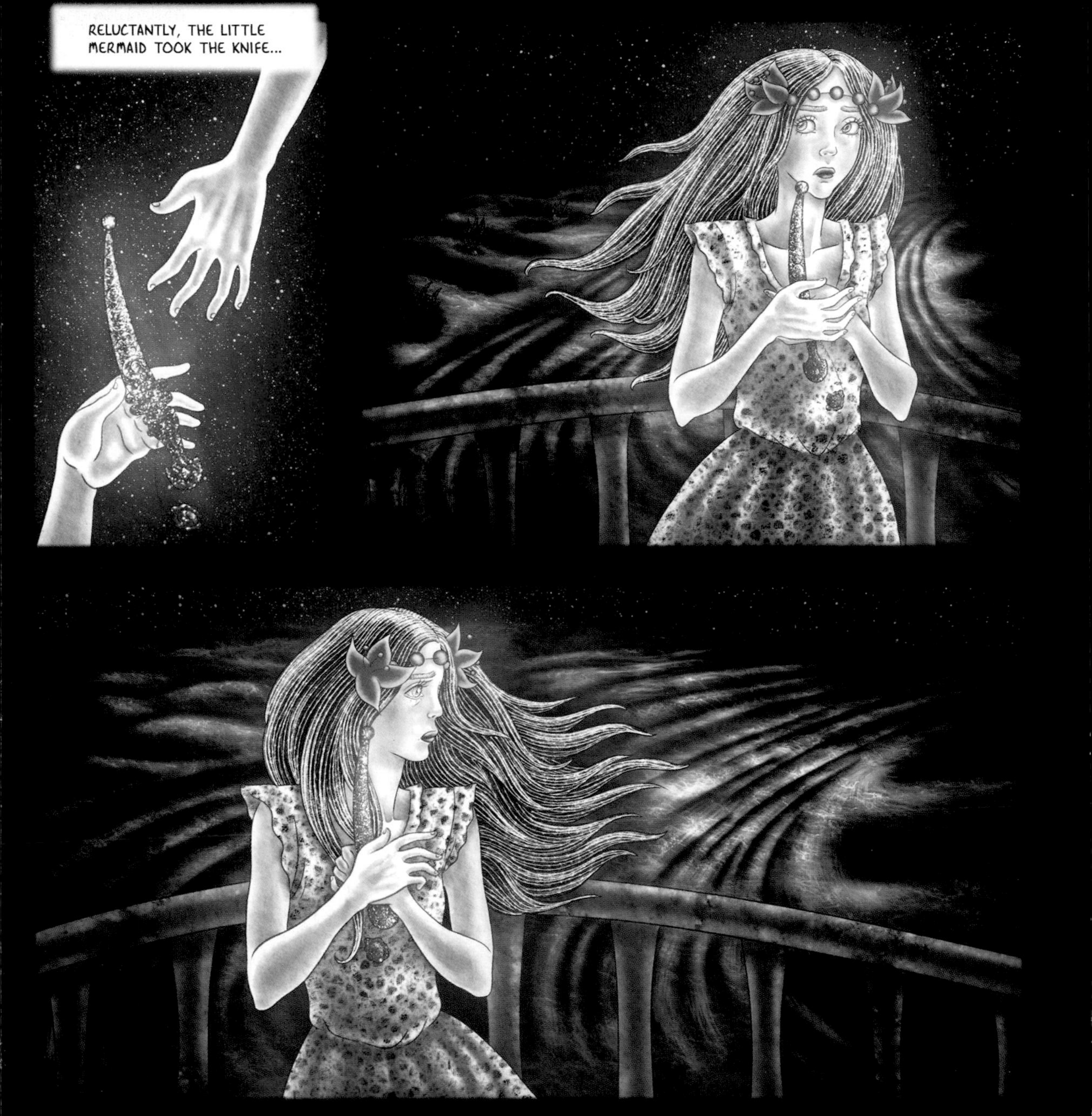
RELUCTANTLY, THE LITTLE MERMAID TOOK THE KNIFE...

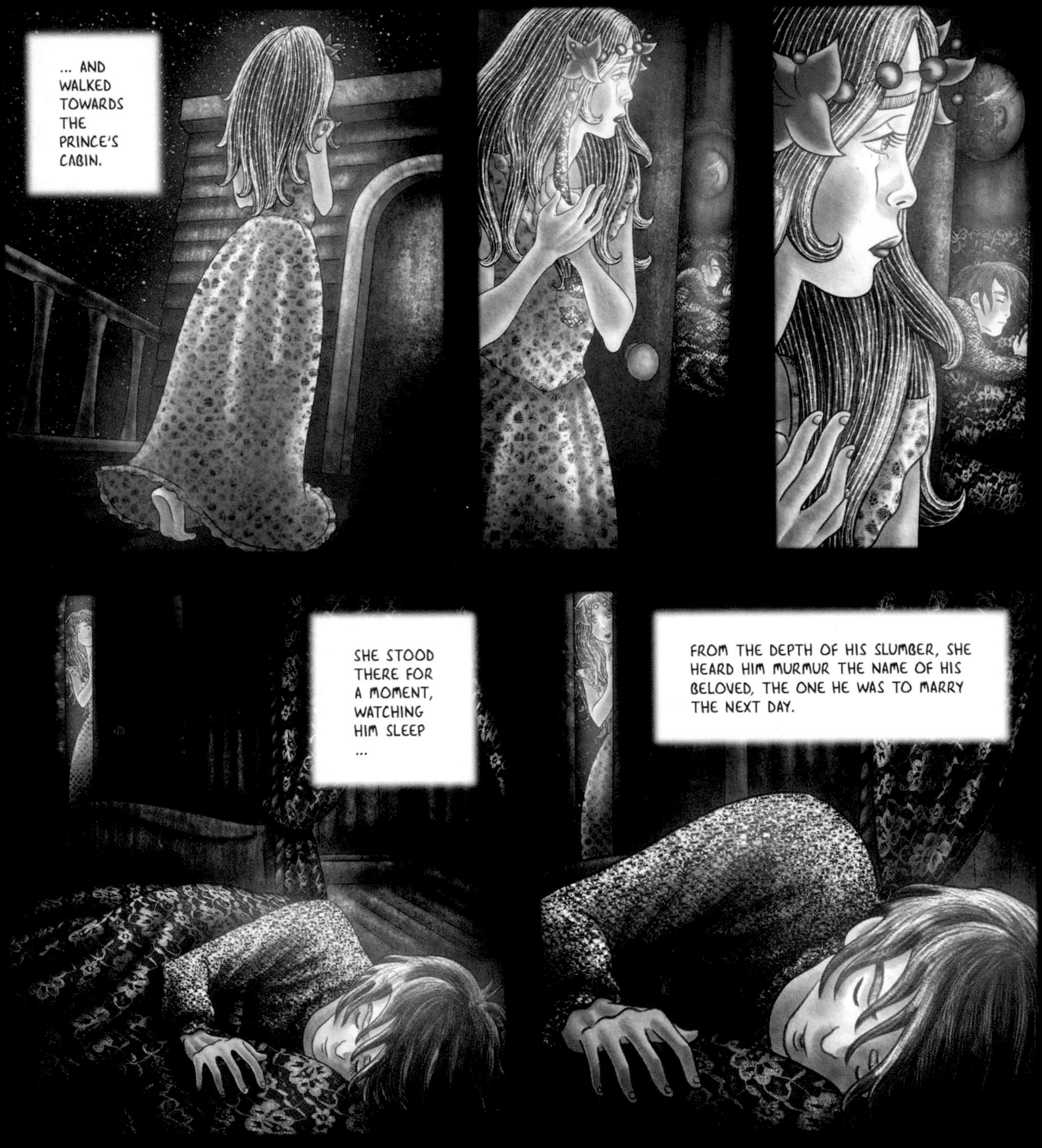
... AND WALKED TOWARDS THE PRINCE'S CABIN.
SHE STOOD THERE FOR A MOMENT, WATCHING HIM SLEEP ...
FROM THE DEPTH OF HIS SLUMBER, SHE HEARD HIM MURMUR THE NAME OF HIS BELOVED, THE ONE HE WAS TO MARRY THE NEXT DAY.

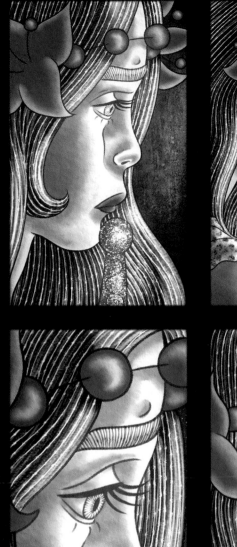

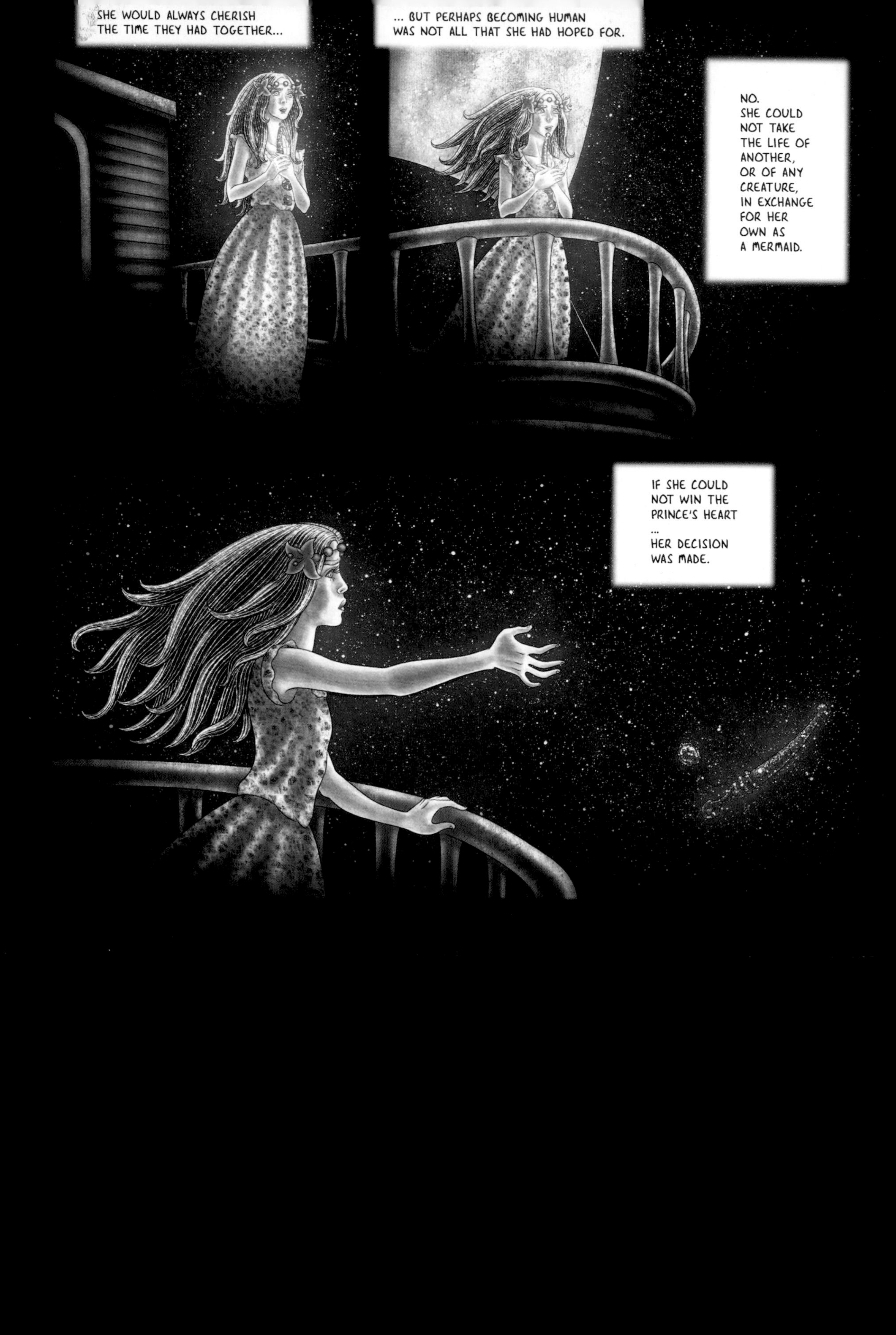
SHE WOULD ALWAYS CHERISH THE TIME THEY HAD TOGETHER...
... BUT PERHAPS BECOMING HUMAN WAS NOT ALL THAT SHE HAD HOPED FOR.
NO. SHE COULD NOT TAKE THE LIFE OF ANOTHER, OR OF ANY CREATURE, IN EXCHANGE FOR HER OWN AS A MERMAID.
IF SHE COULD NOT WIN THE PRINCE'S HEART ... HER DECISION WAS MADE.

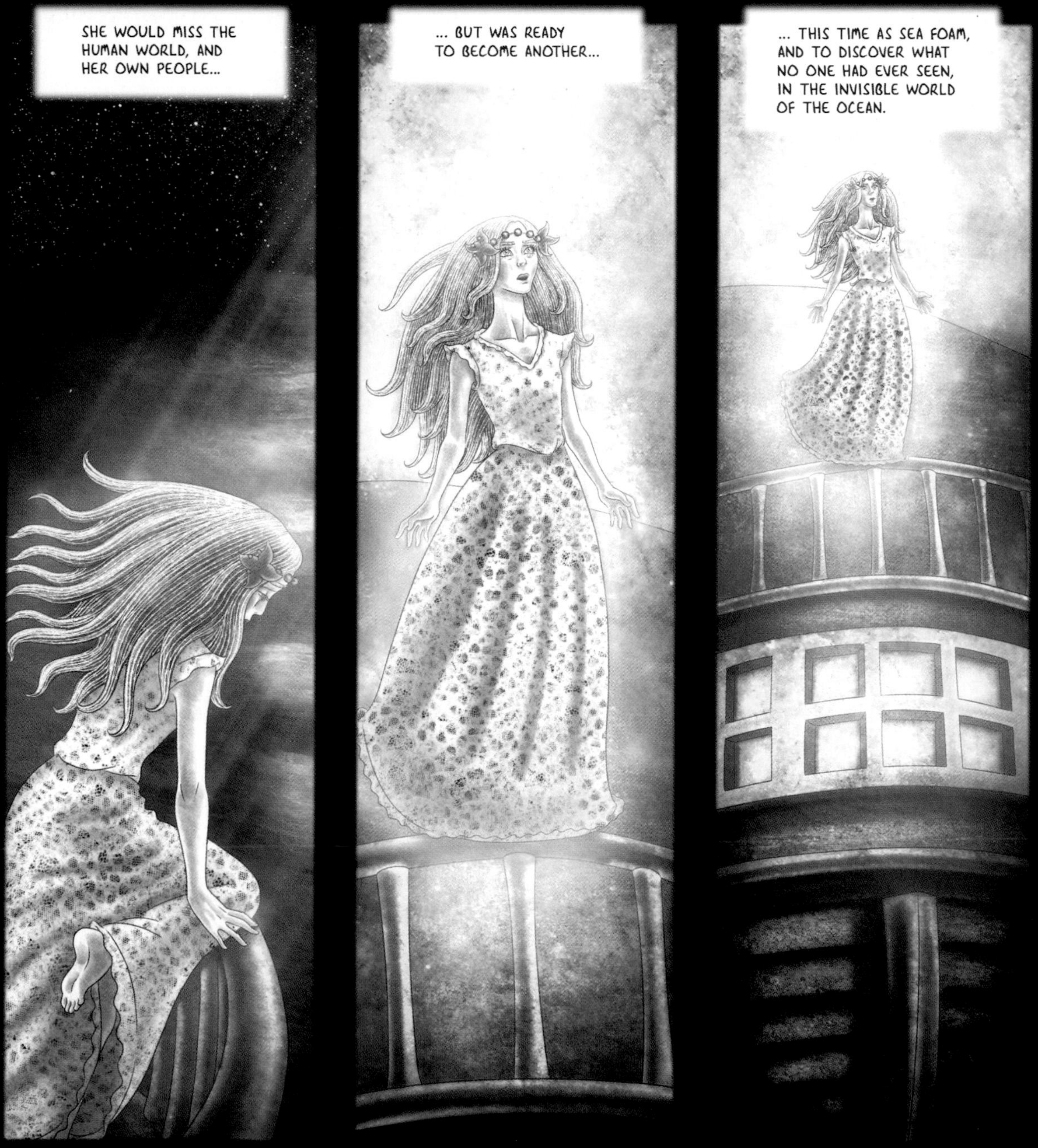
SHE WOULD MISS THE HUMAN WORLD, AND HER OWN PEOPLE...
... BUT WAS READY TO BECOME ANOTHER...
... THIS TIME AS SEA FOAM, AND TO DISCOVER WHAT NO ONE HAD EVER SEEN, IN THE INVISIBLE WORLD OF THE OCEAN.

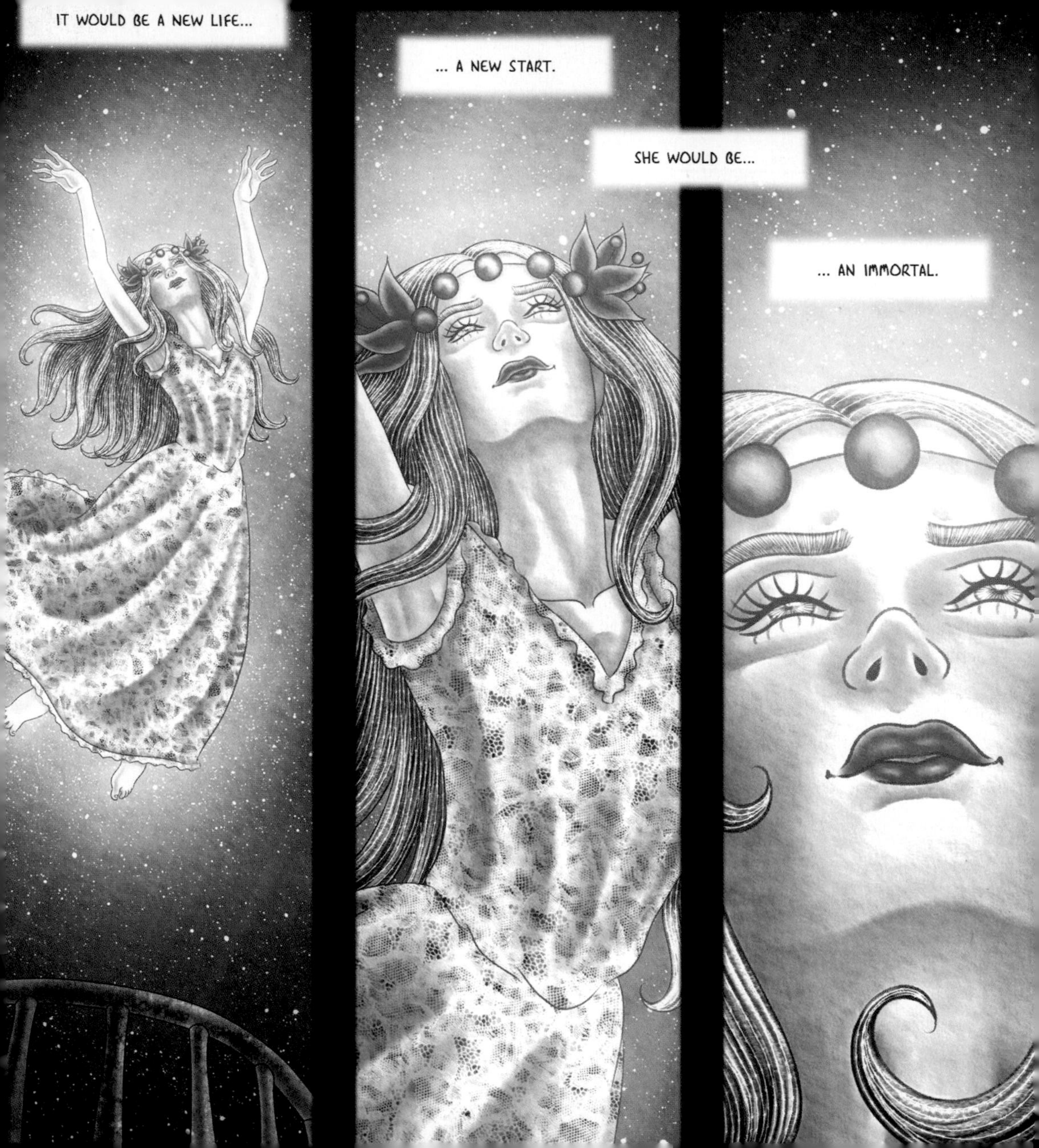
IT WOULD BE A NEW LIFE...
... A NEW START.
SHE WOULD BE...
... AN IMMORTAL.

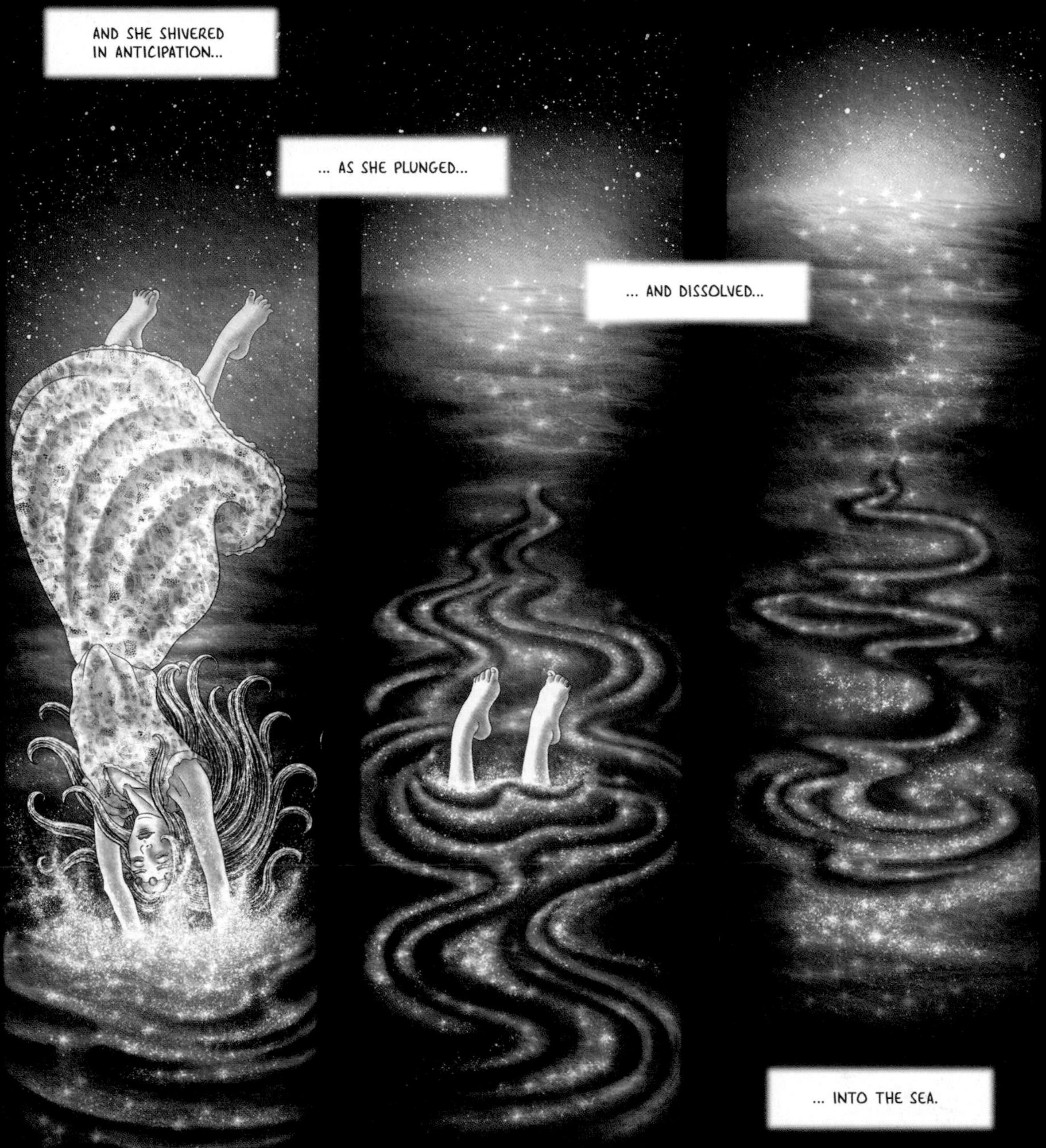
AND SHE SHIVERED IN ANTICIPATION...
... AS SHE PLUNGED...
... AND DISSOLVED...
... INTO THE SEA.

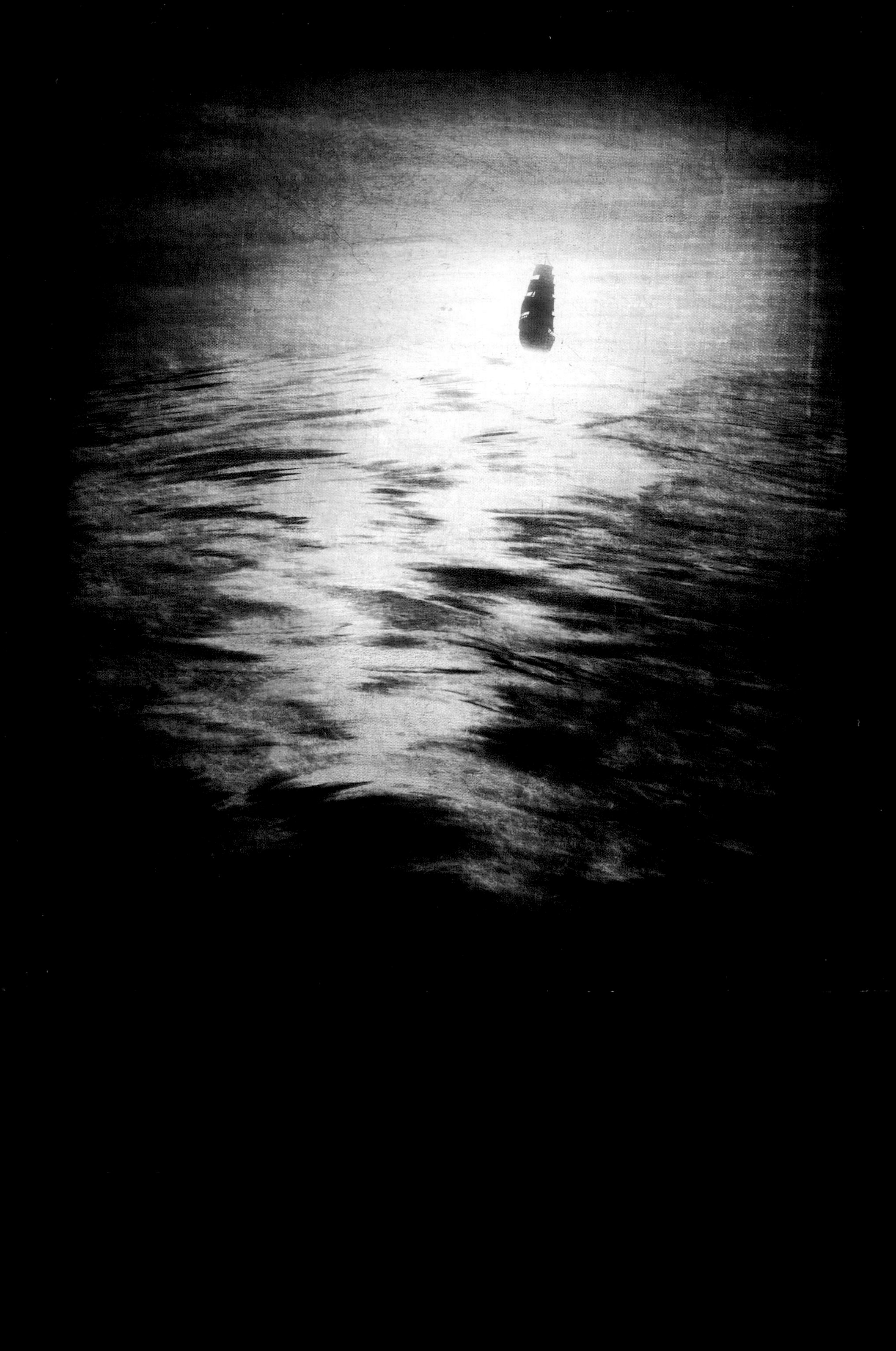

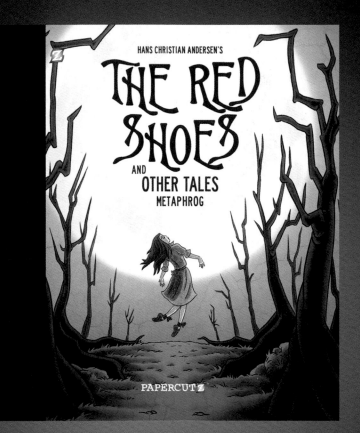

About the Authors:

Metaphrog are John Chalmers and Sandra Marrs, award-winning graphic novelists. They have received multiple Eisner Award nominations and critical acclaim for their Louis series, and Louis — Night Salad was Highly Commended for the Scottish Children's Book Awards 2011. As well as working on their own graphic novels, they have produced an array of illustrations and commissions, and travel extensively to talk about their work and the creative process at festivals, schools, libraries and museums. They are Patrons of Reading at Northfield Academy in Aberdeen and were writers in Residence at the Edinburgh International Book Festival 2015. In 2016, they won The Sunday Herald Scottish Culture Awards for Best Visual Artist. They live and work in Glasgow, Scotland. Visit their website www.metaphrog.com

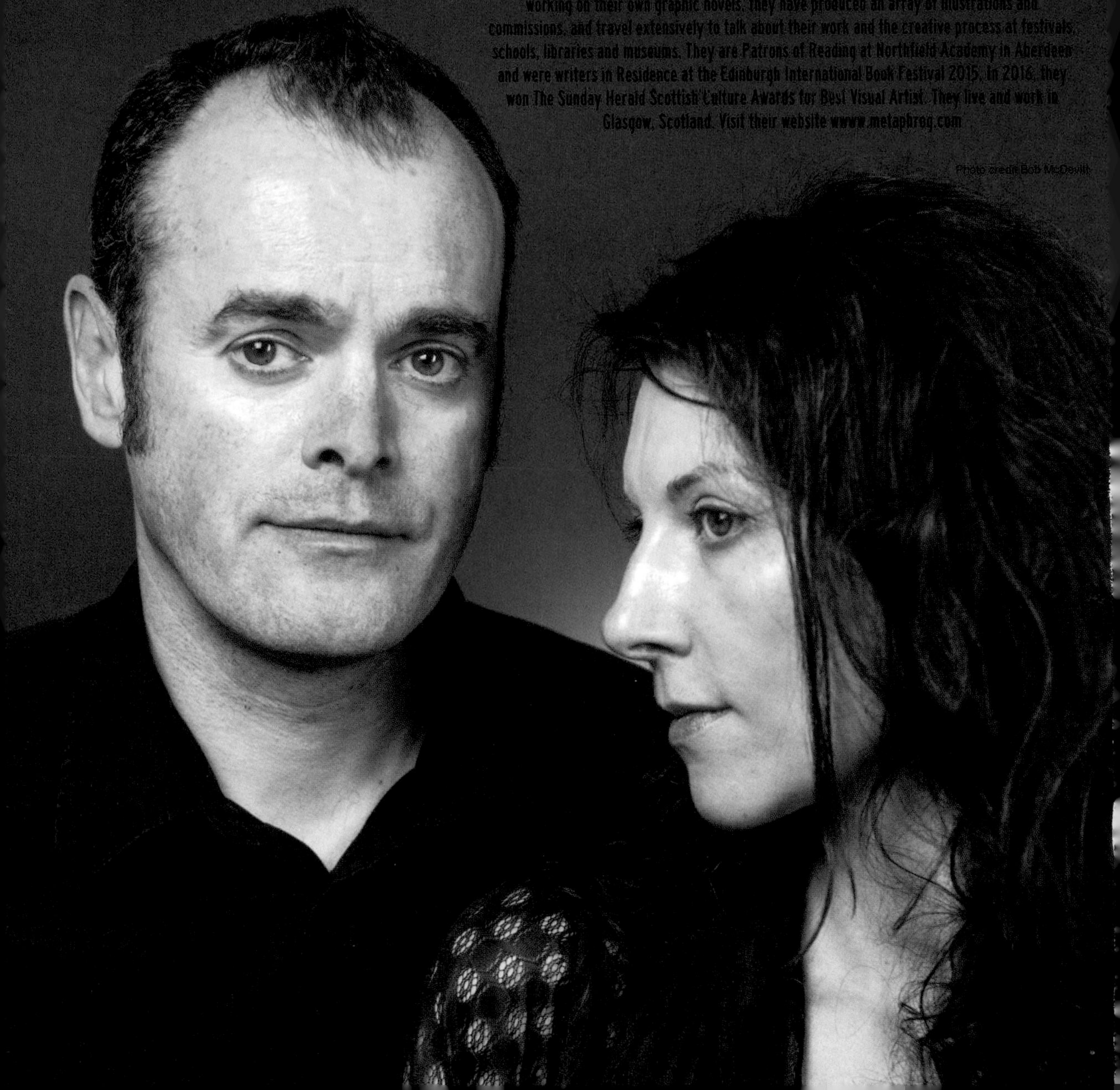

Photo credit Bob McDevitt